The Chosen Profession of Jade Stonecalf

Adventures of a *Fille de Joie*

Trudy Silverheels

with illustrations by

Percy Cabot

ARCHER TRENT, PUBLISHER

Second Edition
2018

ISBN 9780999002940

Dedicated to

Virginia Maureen Ward

CHAPTER I
In Which, Running for my Very Life, I Befriend Another Girl in Desperate Straits

People call me a *whore*, and I suppose I am, but I can't help resenting the label. To me a whore is low class, and I can promise you, I'm anything but low class. A *lady of the night* is what I would prefer to be called or perhaps a *woman of pleasure*. I'm not a drug addict or an alcoholic, which most whores are, at least the ones I've encountered. I wasn't forced into prostitution, and I'm not ashamed of what I do. I knew when I chose this line of work that I could never enjoy the respect of polite society. And yet I felt this to be my true vocation. I still believe that the service I provide is vital.

Let me introduce myself. My name is *Jade Stonecalf*. I'm eighteen years old, almost nineteen. You probably guessed already that I'm Indian, well, not Indian Indian, Native American Indian. My name rather gives it away. Oklahoma is where I was born and brought up. Texas is where I ply my trade.

My decision to go into this profession, instead of medicine or law or something like that, was by no means impulsive. I meditated about it for years. In fact, I believe the idea first entered my head when I was in fifth grade. That's when I learned the word *prostitution* and its definition. I was mightily intrigued that you could actually get paid for giving others the pleasure of your body. It seemed too wonderful to be true. There almost had to be a catch. The catch, of course, is the disapprobation you have to endure from people like my mother: uptight narrow-minded bigots, who think they know what's right for everybody.

I was sixteen when I ran away from home and began earning my own way in the world. But long before that I had got into the practice of offering sexual favors in exchange for whatever material or personal considerations I desired. My first such venture occurred during the summer between sixth and seventh grades. I was a tomboy of the first order, and I wanted more than anything to play baseball with the guys in our neighborhood, but they refused categorically to allow "any dumb girl" into their game. The more I persisted, the more they resisted. So I made them an offer I knew they wouldn't turn down. By the time I got through doing the last of them, it was too dark to play. But for the remainder of the summer, I was a team captain.

In high school I was not allowed to date, but I regularly put out for the boys on our block. And I always got something in return: not necessarily cash money, but something of value. For instance, neighborhood boys often did my chores for me. And I always had the latest CDs, video games, and DVDs to enjoy.

In tenth grade I was permitted for the first time to babysit on Friday and Saturday nights, but only for "respectable" families from our Pentecostal Church. This employment provided me my sole source of financial revenue during my last year at home. The few dollars those young mothers paid me was supplemented nicely by the enormous gratuities their husbands lavished on me when they drove me home at the end of the evening.

I don't want you to think I'm only about the money though. I like men, and I really do find it gratifying to be able to give them such pleasure. If I didn't have to earn a living, I wouldn't mind doing sex for free. Indeed, sometimes I don't charge at all. Like for instance, if I know someone can't afford my regular fee, I usually just tell him it's on the house because he's my five hundredth customer of the week, or maybe I might make up some other silly reason. I think of it as *pro bono* work. Years ago my grandmother got some legal work done *pro bono*, and I fell in love with the concept. So I'm just paying it forward, you might say. Most of my *pro bono* clients are old guys subsisting on minuscule social security checks. Without me to keep them from getting too horny, they'd soon go crazy.

When I launched my career two years ago, I figured that by the time I was twenty-one I'd be able to retire a millionaire. The math is pretty simple. All I should have had to do was save four thousand dollars per week. How hard could that be? My first week on the job I earned more than five thousand. Unfortunately, my calculations did not take into account the fact that as a minor without identification papers, I'd be unable to open a bank account. I was, therefore, forced either to carry my accumulated wealth on my person or to stash it someplace. Neither option proved very satisfactory, for I was robbed over and over again. Still, I lived like a millionaire and never denied myself anything.

I got picked up by the cops a few times before I reached my majority, but on every occasion I was able to persuade my arresting officers to take me somewhere other than to jail. I always do cops for free. But I don't call that *pro bono*; it's more like the cost of doing business.

I even did a female officer once. At first she only wanted to watch me get her partner off; but she got so turned on watching, she then demanded that I do her too. And I absolutely didn't know how, because I had never masturbated in my life and I had never had experience of other girls. But Officer Moreno—I believe that was her name—told me exactly what she wanted me to do, and I did it. Apparently, I did it pretty well too, because thereafter for as long as I was in Dallas, she ran interference for me. I never again had to worry about getting busted.

As my eighteenth birthday approached, I started trying to screw up my courage to return home to ask for my birth certificate and Social Security card. Between customers one night I was so absorbed in rehearsing what I might say to my mother that I was unaware of someone's coming up behind me. Grabbed suddenly by the hair, I was dragged backward ten or fifteen feet, then flung violently into an unlit alleyway between two tall buildings. I crashed into a brick wall and collapse into a pitiful little heap on a rough pavement strewn with broken glass.

My attacker was a notoriously cruel pimp called

Skinny Jay. "I invited you into my office, bitch, to discuss your future. You are seriously cutting into my revenue here lately. That is unacceptable. I think it's time you came to work for me."

"What a cute way to offer somebody a job!" I said, flashing the brightest smile I could muster. I held my left hand out for him to help me up. My right hand, however, was groping for the Bowie knife I carry in a sheath tucked inside my boot top.

Skinny Jay returned my smile with interest, revealing several gold teeth. As he approached, he extended his hand to me. "I'm glad we could come to an understanding so easily. It gives me no pleasure to inflict pain on one as fine as you." He paused and scratched his head, reconsidering, it seemed, the truthfulness of what he had just said. "Well, maybe it does give me a little pleasure, but it's bad business to have my girls too badly marked up."

I let him pull me to my feet and in one fluid motion I sliced him across the belly.

He could not believe that this was happening to him. He stumbled backward, his hands out in front of him to ward off my continuing attack. Nor did I relent. I kept coming at him, slicing fiercely back and forth. I drew more blood with every swipe. The palms of his hands were bleeding, as was the tip of his nose and his right cheek. I could easily have killed him with a single thrust, but I was not prepared to face the kind of trouble that would land me in.

I left him whimpering in fear and pain at the back of the alley. Then I walked as calmly as I could to the Greyhound station. I did not even return to my hotel room for my things, but boarded the first bus leaving town. It mattered not to me which direction I was traveling. Tomorrow or the next day (depending on how

5

seriously I had wounded him), Skinny Jay would be looking for me again, and this time he would have murder in his heart.

Midnight found me sipping coffee in the all-night diner at the bus station in Los Gatos, Texas, two hundred miles from Dallas. I had ordered a hamburger and French fries too, but the food was yet to be put before me. Further down the counter I noticed another Indian girl. At least I suspected that she was Indian (or *Native American* I should remember to say). In Oklahoma, where I come from, Native Americans constitute the vast majority, but since coming to Texas, I had encountered not one other of my race. Till now.

"Hi," I said. "Mind if I sit with you?"

The girl shrugged indifferently. But I was not to be discouraged. I slid my cup down the counter and sat on the stool next to hers.

She signaled the waitress to refill her cup and mine.

This the waitress did, but with an admonishment. "Listen, honey. If you don't order any food, this has got to be your last free refill. You're going to cost me my job."

"Sorry," the girl said. "I'll be leaving after this cup."

When the waitress brought my hamburger, I asked her to cut it in two. I then offered the girl half. "Have some fries too. They always give me more than I can eat."

"Thanks. How come you're being so nice to me?"

"Do I have to have a reason to be nice?"

She didn't respond. How could she? Her mouth was full. The way she wolfed the food down, I was pretty certain she hadn't eaten in a long time. Then she thanked me again and excused herself to go to the restroom. Ten minutes later the loudspeaker announced my bus, but on a whim I decided to let it leave without me. I ordered two more hamburgers and two more orders of fries. When the food arrived, the girl still had not returned; so I went looking for her. I found her weeping uncontrollably in the last stall. It wasn't easy to coax her out or to calm her down, but eventually I managed both tasks. Back at the counter, we introduced ourselves to each other as we tucked into the food.

Her name was *Pamela Pinto*, and she was indeed a Native American. She was approximately the same age as I. She had run away from home to escape "an impossible situation," upon which she refused to elaborate. The bus ticket she had bought in South Dakota had brought her this far. Now she had no more money and nowhere to go.

"You can always sell a little nooky," I suggested.

She blushed a deep scarlet. "I couldn't do that."

"Sure you could. It's the easiest thing in the world. I do it all the time."

"I'd rather die."

I rolled my eyes in exasperation. People can be unbelievably silly. Still, I felt compassionate and very protective toward this girl. Even so, what madness possessed me then to invite her to string along with me?

"Really? You mean it?" She was so relieved I thought she was going to hug me. In the next instant, however, a look of alarm came over her face. "You're not a lesbian, are you? 'Cause I'm not into shit like that."

I had to laugh. In my entire life I had never been friends with another girl. I didn't understand girls, didn't begin to know how their minds work, or how to relate to them. Men I could read like a book, but girls were a total mystery to me. "Relax, kiddo. I don't want anything from you. I'm just trying to be your friend."

From the waitress, we got walking directions to a nearby motel. Then I left a fat gratuity on the counter by way of saying thank you.

Generous tipping is the right thing to do for more reasons than one. In the first place, waitresses work a lot harder than I do and earn a fraction of what I make. Then too from a purely practical standpoint, it's smart to have people remember you in a friendly way. You might have to pass this way again someday.

A neon sign in the front window of the motel office announced, "No Vacancy." So we continued walking along the highway toward the center of town. Eventually we came to a small hotel. A hundred years earlier the Gibson Arms had probably been a quite-elegant establishment, but now it was in shabby disrepair and badly in need of paint. We found only one vacancy there, which, unfortunately, was not a double. Neither Pam nor I were keen to share a bed, but there was no choice, unless one of us wanted to sleep on the floor. I showered first and was sound asleep by the time she finished her shower and crawled in beside me.

In the morning we had to put back on our dirty clothes from the day before. I hate ever having to do that, but this was an exceptional circumstance. Downstairs in the hotel coffee shop we devoured a huge breakfast and two or three cups of coffee each, then set out afoot to explore the town while waiting for the stores to open.

Along the main highway I spotted several likely bars. I had an idea I wanted to try out. In Dallas I had worked a street corner, from which I usually managed to do two tricks an hour. Theoretical, I should have been able to do three in that time or even four, but when I'm charging two hundred and fifty dollars for the experience, I feel like I ought to give a guy his money's worth and not rush him. I had had a cell phone too in order that my regulars could call me up to make dates. But that phone had gone into a trash can in the Dallas bus station early last evening. God! Was that really only twelve hours ago? It felt like a hundred years had passed.

Leaving Dallas, I initially imagined that I should simply start over in another big city (Houston most likely or possibly New Orleans). Then as I rode through one small town after another, a revised business plan began to take shape in my mind. There were still details to be worked out, but I was eager to get started. In some ways, what I now intended to do would be even riskier than working a street corner. But if I could somehow neutralize or even minimize the police threat, then the rewards could be enormous. In the first place, I could charge a lot less and still earn vastly more each night. Perhaps of even greater importance, I'd be enjoying myself more and providing pleasure to many more men than had previously been possible. Maybe I could yet achieve millionaire status by age twenty-one.

At ten o'clock Pam and I were waiting outside the front doors when Beall's Department Store opened for business. We picked out new clothes (a few complete changes each consisting of miniskirts and western shirts), new luggage (one small suitcase each), scads of sexy underwear, cowboy hats, and for Pam a pair of fringed squaw boots to replace her frayed sneakers. My own cowboy boots were still like new. The bill came to just over seven hundred dollars. I paid with cash.

Pam was astounded. She gushed her gratitude, which fact only served to make me uncomfortable.

"Please don't say anything more about it," I told her. "If you're going to hang out with me, you have to look cute."

Already I had begun thinking of Pam as a younger relative to be protected and taken care of. That she was actually older than I by a few weeks did not seem possible, and yet her driver's license indicated that this was indeed the case.

What a pair we made! Who would have believed that such a worldly young woman as I with carnal knowledge of thousands of men could find anything in common with a naïve virgin? From the very first, I felt a strong affinity for her, and apparently, she was rapidly becoming attached to me as well. She took my hand and held it as we walked back to our hotel.

"I'm so glad I ran into you last night," Pam told me as we let ourselves into our room. "Thank you for rescuing me. If you give me a little time to get used to the idea, I'll do whatever you say in order to pay you back."

"Not necessary," I assured her. "I'm no more a lesbian than you are."

Pam's face went suddenly quite red. "I didn't mean that. I was talking about doing what you do so I can earn my own money."

"Forget it. You're not cut out for that kind of thing. I suggested it last night before I knew you. Doing sex for money suits me, but it's not for you. I can see that now."

"I'm willing to learn. And I want to pay my own way."

"I don't want you to. I just want you to be my friend. Okay? I never had a friend before. Keep me company when I'm not working."

Pam shrugged. "If that's what you really want."

"It is," I said firmly. And I meant it.

We took our noon meal at the Cattlemen's Steak House that day, and not surprisingly, every man in the place was gaping at us. I was used to attracting that kind of attention, but it was a new experience for Pam. I had restyled her hair, taught her how to apply makeup to enhance her natural good looks, and most significantly, I had insisted that she not wear her extremely unbecoming glasses, without which, unfortunately, she was almost blind.

After lunch we went first to an optometrist to ask about getting Pam contact lenses. Then we visited an optician to place the order. The prescription would be ready in one week, we were told. In the meantime, Pam would just have to stumble around in a myopic haze. I wanted her to start immediately thinking of herself as pretty. And she was indeed pretty. Today she was pretty. Last night she would hardly have warranted a second glance. The transformation was nothing less than miraculous.

At the First National Bank I had Pam open a checking account and a savings account, for I still had no identification papers and she did. I gave her seventeen thousand dollars to deposit. Her contribution to our partnership, I suggested, might be to manage the money I made for us both. I confided to her my secret ambition to become a millionaire at a very young age.

"Maybe we should start investing in the stock market," she ventured timidly.

"I don't know anything about it," I confessed. "Do you?"

"No, but I can do some research if this town has a public library. I don't need glasses to read."

"Would it help to have a computer?" I asked.

"Sure. If I had Internet."

So we bought a laptop that afternoon and a USB mobile Internet receptor. Then as an afterthought I picked out two smart phones in order that we might stay in touch at all times. I intended to leave her at the hotel when I went to work each night, but I wanted her to be able to reach me if she needed me.

Richard Bach in his book *Illusions* observed, "Your friends will know you better the first minute you meet than your acquaintances will know you in a thousand years." And so it was with Pam and me. We had been together less than twenty-four hours, and already I could no longer imagine my life without her. She had become a part of me, and I was a part of her. Together we could conquer the world, or so it felt to us.

CHAPTER II
In Which I Am Paid a Visit by the Chief of Police

The first bar I checked out that afternoon was managed by a woman. I simply turned around and walked back outside into the sunlight, where Pam was waiting for me.

"What's wrong? You weren't in there two minutes."

"This isn't the right place."

The next place wasn't the right place either. Before I could even launch my rehearsed spiel, the bartender demanded to see my ID, which, of course, I was unable to produce. I was discouraged, but I decided to try once more. If, this time, it didn't work out, I'd head back to Oklahoma to collect my identity papers. Then I'd start over. I was still convinced that my idea was a good one.

Entering the pretentiously named Lone Star Saloon, I found it necessary to pause just inside the door to allow my eyes to adjust to the darkness. I was struck by how very cool it was in there. And at this early hour, it was empty of customers. The only person I saw was the bartender. Fat and bald, he was greedily devouring me with his eyes. Bingo! This was a perfect setup.

I climbed up onto a bar stool immediately in front of the man, and tossing a condom pack down on the bar between us, I showed him my warmest smile. "I have a business proposition to put to you. And while we chat, I want you to be thinking about how you and I can put that Trojan to good use."

He was practically drooling. "You have my full attention."

Thirty minutes later I walked out into the sunshine to find Pam waiting anxiously for me.

"How did it go?"

"Couldn't have been better."

On the way back to the hotel, I filled Pam in on the details of my arrangement with Lou, the owner and manager of the Lone Star. He had agreed to close his doors to the general public this coming Friday night and host a private party for a select group of discreet patrons. I would be providing the entertainment. Lou was expecting to sell an awfully lot of beer and many dozens of condoms as well. This weekend promised to be almost as profitable for him as for me. He had already enjoyed a free sample of what I'd be selling at the party, and he could expect more of the same on Friday night after closing.

My only concern was the local constabulary. But Lou, being the brother-in-law of the chief of police, assured me that we had nothing to fear on that account. I assumed, therefore, that I should be hearing from the chief himself sometime between now and Friday. I fully expected to show my gratitude in the usual way. It's always smart to have the cops on your side; so I go out of my way to insure that they feel appreciated.

But what should I do for the rest of the week? Today was only Wednesday. I hated to remain idle for two whole days. At twilight Pam and I walked out to the edge of town to eat supper at a roadside café associated with a busy, sprawling truck stop. Over chicken-fried steaks and French fries I scoped out the possibilities for earning a little extra income.

Believe me when I tell you, there is not a man in the world who wouldn't find me desirable, unless, of course, he's totally gay. I'm not bragging. It's just a fact. In anybody's book, I'm a perfect ten, which is at least three points above most girls in my line of work. That's why I can get away with asking so much. In Dallas I had consistently got paid two and a half times what my closest competitors were charging. And no man ever complained that my price was too high.

Pam received as many lecherous glances that night in the café as did I. Her new look showed her to be outrageously sexy. At first it made her uncomfortable to be the object of such unaccustomed attention, but gradually she began to warm to it and eventually developed the habit of kissing her fingertips and then wiggling them inconspicuously at any man she noticed leering at her. But if one ever got up the nerve to ask her out, she would inevitably decline "with regrets." She disappointed a lot of men that night, but she hurt no one's feelings. "Maybe some other time," she would tell them. Nor had I taught her how to do this; she had figured it out on her own, and I quite admired her for having done so.

Several times I left her alone and followed some

trucker or another out to his rig, where I made my pitch in private. I saw the inside of perhaps a dozen sleeper compartments that night. And the next morning I was able to hand Pam a fat wad of bills to deposit. Unfortunately, we had rather over-stayed our welcome at the café. I had allowed avarice to cloud my judgment. We should have left much earlier; then we might have returned a few nights later to do it again. As things stood, we were "not wanted on these premises again." Oh, well, live and learn.

The chief of police, whose name was *Harold Taggart*, showed up for his lagniappe on Thursday afternoon. I was surprised that he was so very old. I had expected a man about the same age as Lou, who was probably between forty-five and fifty, but the chief was at least a generation older than that. He was tall and lanky with short, straight gray hair. He was sloppy too. He wore his uniform poorly, and he slouched. I suppose these observations are not terribly important, but I'm just telling you what struck me about him at the time. I also noticed that his skin was extremely sallow. I guessed that he was not in good health. The fact that his breath was so vile seemed to further support my suspicion.

In any event, Pam let him into our room. Then I sent her away, saying I'd call her later when I was free. As soon as the door shut behind her, I began getting out of my clothes. Chief Taggart watched with keen interest, but he made no move to undress himself. Completely naked now, I threw myself onto the bed and motioned him to join me.

"You are without doubt the loveliest creature I have ever laid eyes on. But I wonder whether you have the skills to help me."

"If I can't help you, nobody can. I'm the best

16

there is. How exactly would you like me to help you?"

He declined to answer but sat on the edge of the bed and began exploring my body with his hands. My own hand groped instinctively at the front of his trousers.   Quickly I came to understand that he was afflicted with erectile dysfunction, a condition with which I had been confronted before. It is not nearly as much a challenge as you might think. With enough careful attention, an impotent prick can sometimes be coaxed to stand erect again. But even if that small miracle does not occur, I can still help the sufferer to a more-than-satisfying climax with my hands. I've done it countless times. The trick is to employ lots of lotion and pull hand over hand off the end of the penis. It is a technique that works even when the organ in question is totally limp.

In the end, that's how I had to get Taggart off. Briefly he was able to achieve an erection, but he lost it as I was trying to fit him with a condom. I helped him to come on my breasts.   Men hate to see their semen wasted by being spilled on the floor or the sheets. If they can't get it inside me, they at least want it on me. In any event, Taggart went away a happy man, but not before warning me that he had received a complaint about my truck-stop activities the night before.

"After the big event Friday night, you need to move on. You can't make this town your permanent home. I'm sorry to have to say that, because I'd really like the chance to do this again."

"My roommate has ordered contacts from TSO. They'll be here next Monday. Will that be soon enough for us to leave? I won't do anything else to cause you embarrassment. I promise."

"Monday will be fine. And in a few months, if you feel like drifting back through here, I don't think that would be too much of a problem. You could even hold another blowout at Lou's place if you felt like it. But stay away from the truck-stop. The old biddy that runs the café there is a holy roller, and she has you pegged for a 'servant of Satan.'"

Still quite naked, I shook Taggart's hand, then kissed his cheek in farewell. (I had wiped his semen off my chest with a damp towel as he was getting dressed.) He patted my bottom one last time and bid me good luck.

CHAPTER III
In Which I Get Back to Business

The Lone Star Saloon was packed to overflowing on Friday night. Lou's patrons seemed primarily to be farmers and ranchers, cowboys, roughnecks, and construction workers, but there were also present a number of merchants and professional men. I immediately recognized in the crowd Pam's optometrist and the owner of the Gibson Arms. The music was deafeningly loud, and the atmosphere was electric. I smiled to myself. This was going to be fun, and I was going to clean up. I had never done a gangbang before. You might expect that I would be nervous, but I wasn't. I was high on anticipation.

I had a quick word with Lou. Then with his help, I climbed up on top of the bar. I was wearing my usual work uniform to which I had now added a pink straw cowboy hat. My getup consisted of a blue denim miniskirt, a western shirt with pearl snaps, and fancy cowboy boots. Underneath I wore lacy bikini panties but no bra. I never wear a bra when I'm working. At least half the eyes in the room were already fixed on me. I removed my panties and waved them over my head.

"Who wants some pussy?" I shouted at the top of my voice.

The immediate uproar could easily have been heard in the next county. Dozens of men rushed forward, shoving and pushing each other to be first.

"Whoa!" I shouted, putting my palm out like a traffic cop. "There's plenty to go around. But this can't be a free-for-all. It has to be orderly."

Lou unplugged the jukebox so I wouldn't have to shout.

"Here's how we're going to do this," I explained when I finally had silence. "You guys are going to form a line behind these two heroes." I indicated two decorated marines standing at the bar. "They're going to go first. That's what you leathernecks do best, isn't it? Lead the way?"

"Yes, ma'am!" The two marines answered enthusiastically and in unison.

"Well, for you and anyone else in uniform tonight, it's my treat. The rest of you fellas should have your money in hand. Sixty dollars. Make it three twenties please, so I don't have to spend precious time counting ones and fives and tens. By the way, sixty dollars is a fraction of what I usually charge. If you don't have that much cash on you, Lou has very considerately installed a brand new ATM by the front door. He also has condoms for sale at the bar in case the machine in the bathroom runs out. Everybody uses protection. No exceptions."

There was some shuffling about as men began to queue up.

"One more thing: you only get five minutes each. I hate the necessity for that. But if I'm going to do everybody here, I have to set a time limit, else I won't get done till noon tomorrow. Five minutes, for your information, is to the count of three hundred. Bystanders can help by counting aloud."

"Is there a prize for finishing fastest?" someone behind me asked.

"What a great idea!" I exclaimed. "How's this? Whoever comes in the least amount of time tonight can take his time with me tomorrow night for free."

"Meaning exactly what?" The anonymous voice again.

So I spelled it out in unambiguous terms. "The winner tonight gets a date with me tomorrow night. He can do anything to me he wants, and I'll do anything he asks for as long as it takes to give him full satisfaction. Now, somebody please help me down, and let's get this party started."

My two marines each extended a hand, and together they lifted me down. Most of the tables nearby were round with center pedestals. They wouldn't do at all to support me in this endeavor. But out in the middle of the room I spotted a sturdy four-legged table built to seat six. I hoisted myself up onto the nearest end and sat on the edge with my feet dangling off. I then unsnapped my shirt to expose my breasts, which I jiggled teasingly with my hands.

"Lock and load, guys. I'm ready."

As zippers came down, I scooted back a bit, then reclined fully and I brought my feet up to hook the heels of my boots on the edge of the table. My knees were wide apart; my bare pussy, fully exposed to the room. In my purse, which was large enough to carry all the loot I expected to be leaving with later, I had also brought several tubes of K-Y jelly.

The first marine thrust his erect penis into me and began pumping in and out. The men in line behind him and others standing about watching began to mark the passing seconds with a loud chant. "One, two, three, four, five—" He finished in seventy-five seconds. His buddy beat him by twenty seconds. The third man in line was a grossly obese rancher almost seven feet tall. He took considerably longer. Indeed, he seemed to be in danger of running out of time; so I helped him by tightly clamping my vaginal muscles at the same instant I lightly touch his scrotum with my fingernails. I had to reach awkwardly beneath my own hip to do this, but I had no intention of letting anyone go away unsatisfied. It's a matter of professional pride. The dear man came within seconds of my doing that.

Forty-five minutes later, I absolutely had to take a break. My lower back was killing me, and my throat was parched. I got down from the table and stretched a bit this way and that. Someone offered me a beer, but I refused it. Native Americans are genetically predisposed to alcoholism, or so I had always heard, and I preferred not to take a chance of wrecking my future by becoming too fond of drink. I asked instead for a soda pop, then chug-a-lugged it when handed a Sprite. I don't really like Sprites. I much prefer root beer, but root beer is hardly ever served in bars.

Back to work, and this time I went more than an hour before having to take another break. I only called a halt when I could no longer bear the discomfort of a distended bladder. I excused myself to go the restroom, and predictably, someone asked if I needed any help.

"No, I've been doing this by myself for lots of years, but you're welcome to watch if you want to."

No fewer than twenty men followed me and crowded into the ladies' room with me, but the stall was so narrow that most of my would-be witnesses ended up seeing nothing very interesting. In case I have not yet made it abundantly clear, I was the only female in Lou's establishment that night. That's why it was okay for those men to enter the ladies' room.

"I could make a pretty good living charging money to let people watch me pee," I joked as I washed my hands before returning to my table.

The later it got, the longer I managed to endure between breaks. The evening lasted almost six hours, in which time I took only four breaks. I earned more than I ever had before in a single night. Had I collected from those two marines and from Lou's doorkeeper, whom I also did for free, I should have topped the five thousand dollar mark. Oh, yes. I did Lou himself again too.

The prize for fastest finish went to a slender, good-looking young cowboy, who achieved orgasm in less than half a minute. He made me laugh by confessing that he'd done without for so long, it was a wonder he lasted twenty-five seconds. I promised to meet him back here tomorrow night at seven o'clock for our date. I forgot to ask him his name.

Several different men offered to drive me home, but having seen how much beer they had all drunk, I demurred. I asked Lou to call me a taxi instead. The fare was only five dollars, but of course, I gave the driver a nice tip. I paid with a twenty-dollar bill and let him keep the change. I even flirted with him a bit. I had no doubt he'd remember me fondly if ever we met again.

Pam was up waiting for me when I let myself in.

So glad was she to see me, she hugged me to her and seemed reluctant to turn me loose. I had told her once quite truthfully that I had never before had a girlfriend. Now it dawned on me how much I really valued her. Indeed, I felt so overwhelmed with gratitude for having met her that I kissed her on the lips. Embarrassed, she quickly stepped away from me and sat down on the edge of the bed to count the loot. I sat down beside her, but not so close as to make her uncomfortable. As if to reassure me that she was not upset with me, she briefly laid her hand on my shoulder.

"I had a good night tonight," I told her. "But god, I hurt!"

Pam giggled. "I'll bet your pussy's sore?"

"My back. It's killing me. Next time I do this, I'm taking a pillow to put under me."

"I'll give you a massage. But don't you want to take a shower first?"

"Yeah," I said, getting to my feet. "I can't believe how tired I am."

After my shower I felt so refreshed, I urged Pam to get dressed again in order that we might go out to eat. I was famished. The only nourishment I had ingested in the last eight hours was a single soft drink. We went to the bus-station diner for steak and eggs. In that small town, we likely would have found no other restaurant open at that hour.

Back in our room, I stripped down to my panties and lay on the bed face down. Pam, in panties and bra, straddled my thighs and began kneading the muscles of my lower back. I must have fallen asleep while she worked on me, for my next awareness was of bright sunshine streaming into the room through the gauzy curtains. I was now lying on my back, and Pam, sound asleep, was snuggled against me, her cheek lying on my

bare breast. How sweet she looked! And how innocent!
She could easily have passed for a thirteen-year-old.

We breakfasted at the City Café downtown. This
was a favorite haunt of farmers and ranchers.   I
recognized a number of faces from the night before.
Ever the soul of discretion, however, I pretended not to
notice them. Only if spoken to first, do I address a client
of mine in public.   I have to assume that most men
would prefer that it not be general knowledge that they
are acquainted with me.

When the bank opened that morning, we
deposited four thousand dollars.   Only nine hundred
seventy-nine thousand to go.

Now, you are probably wondering how I could so
easily have given my unconditional trust to a strange girl
about whom I knew almost nothing. I cannot begin to
put into words my reasons. I simply know that it felt like
the right thing to do. I also knew that, were she to
betray my confidence and rip me off, then that fact itself
would devastate me far more than the loss of the money.
In a way, then, this was to be the proof of her character
and the verification of her loyalty.   Of course, if she
failed the test, it might be weeks or months before I
found out. But believe it or not, I gave the matter hardly
a moment's consideration.

I cannot recall how exactly we passed the day. It
never really mattered what we were doing or where we
were. Our greatest pleasure was each other's company.
I was never bored with Pam, and I'd bet a thousand
dollars that she'd tell you the same about me.   We
laughed and giggled like high school girls, shared
amusing stories (gossip about celebrities mostly),
compared likes and dislikes in pop music, and discussed
movies we had seen or longed to see.

At seven o'clock that evening I entered the Lone

Star Saloon to meet my date. The place was again crowded and noisy, but nothing like the night before. From the back of the room, I heard someone shout, "Pocahontas!" I waved in the general direction whence the voice had come. Little did I know that this was to be my new name.

I stepped up to the bar and asked Lou whether he had seen my cowboy yet tonight.

"He was here a while ago. I think he might be in the restroom. Want a Coke or a Sprite?"

"Sure," I said. "Make it a Coke."

Sipping my soft drink, I was quickly surrounded by men vying for my attention. I recognized a couple of them from the night before, but I was pretty certain that the others were new to me. I have an amazing memory for the men I have had sex with. I can't always recall their names, but I never forget their faces. Well, almost never. There are exceptions to every rule.

"Excuse me, gents." My date had come out of the men's room, and taking my arm, he was attempting to extricate me from my other admirers. "She's all mine tonight."

A few of the men in the circle seemed about to take exception.

"He's right," I apologized, hopping down from my stool. "I came in tonight just to meet him. But there'll be other times, I promise. Bye."

Brent Driskoll—for that was the young man's name, I now learned—drove me out of town a few miles to a broken-down little ranch he was proud to call his own. I had been prepared to take him back to the hotel, but this was preferable for many reasons.

"Are you hungry?" he asked, as we entered the house by the kitchen door. "Or do you want to get right down to business?"

26

Home-made *chili con carne* bubbling away in a slow cooker on the counter top smelled so heavenly, I didn't even try to resist it. From the refrigerator Brent put out crackers, yellow cheese, and iced tea. Then we sat at the kitchen table, which was covered with a flower-print oil cloth, and we enjoyed a leisurely supper, chatting pleasantly all the while. I've never meet anyone I didn't find interesting in one way or another. But Brent Driskoll was an absolutely fascinating man. Don't get me wrong. I wasn't in danger of falling in love with him. But I really did like him a lot.

Consider his story; I think you'll understand what I mean. Brent inherited this ranch from his great grandfather, and he had always hoped someday to retire here. But first he planned a career in the navy. He actually became a SEAL. However, after being badly wounded in a combat operation in Afghanistan, he received a medical discharge. Now he was trying to turn his hobby ranch into a successful business.

Downing my tea, I glanced at my watch. "It's getting late. Why don't you show me the bedroom now?"

Believe me, I treat all my customers like they're special. I try to make every sexual encounter with me memorable. But I outdid myself with Brent Driskoll. I was inspired. If there exists a patron saint of prostitutes, I'm sure I made her proud that night.

When Brent took me home, I gave him my phone number, but not without reminding him, "It's always a business doing pleasure with you."

CHAPTER IV
In Which I Learn the Meaning of True Love

I had promised Chief Taggart that I would do nothing else to cause him embarrassment. At the time I had assumed that keeping my promise would require me to refrain from turning any more tricks in his town. Good to my word, I had made no further effort to seek out new business. However, on Sunday afternoon when I went down to the hotel office to give notice that that we would be checking out the following day, Mr Gibson (the owner/manager) expressed a desire to avail himself of my professional services. He had participated in the gangbang on Friday night, but before I left town, he yearned for the opportunity to have me again in a more leisurely fashion. I could see no way this might ever get back to Taggart.

"Two fifty," I told him. "I'll make it the most-incredible experience of your life."

"I don't doubt that for a moment. When's a good time for you?" he asked.

"Now wouldn't be a bad time if you'll give me five minutes to tell my roommate. She's waiting for me go someplace with her. Or I can catch you after we get back."

"She could join us," he suggested hopefully. "How much extra would that be?"

I shook my head. "She's not in the business, Mr Gibson."

"Oh, well," he sighed. "I just thought—I mean—she's really cute."

"I'll tell her you said so. She'll be flattered, I'm sure. But she wouldn't be comfortable doing the things I do."

"Probably for the best. Both of you at once would almost certainly give me a heart attack."

I made an appointment to return later when Mr Gibson's brother could relieve him at the front desk. That way we wouldn't be interrupted by someone's ringing the buzzer for service. Then as previously planned, Pam and I went looking for a Dairy Queen she had heard about on the other side of town. We had both been craving chili dogs and vanilla milkshakes, and while one vanilla milkshake is pretty much the same as any other, no other chili dog in the world can compare to one from Dairy Queen. On this point we were in total agreement. Nor had we any difficulty finding our way to this destination.

"We need to be back by six," I informed Pam as we unwrapped our chili dogs. "I have a date with Mr Gibson."

Pam was shocked. "Mr Gibson, the manager of

the hotel?"

"The same. He asked me when I went down to the office."

"But, Jade, he's old. He's almost bald."

I laughed. "He may be losing his hair, but he hasn't lost his hankering for sex. I've done guys a lot older than Mr Gibson. What about Chief Taggart?"

"Yeah, but he's creepy. Mr Gibson seems so nice."

"He is nice, Pam. He wanted to do you too, by the way. I told him no. I hope that's alright."

"Of course it's alright. He could be my grandfather."

"I suppose you're going to tell me now you've never had sex with your grandfather."

"Once or twice maybe."

Now I was shocked. "Seriously?"

"No, silly, I was just going along with your joke."

On the walk back to the hotel, Pam asked whether I would be entertaining Mr Gibson in our room or elsewhere.

"I don't know yet. Probably we'll do it in his apartment behind the office. Why?"

"I was just wondering if it would be okay if I watched. I'd like to know what you do. I mean, I know what you do, but don't know how you do it. I can't picture it in my mind."

Nothing else that Pam might have said would have surprised me more. In fact, I was so surprised by her unusual request that I was momentarily speechless."

"Do you think Mr Gibson would object?"

"Mmm! My guess would be that he would find that just kinky enough to be exciting. I can ask him. I know he wants to fuck you."

"I don't want to do that. I don't want him to touch me at all. I just want to watch."

Our Mr Gibson's first name, we learned, was *Al*. His brother's name was *Joel*. Joel was older by several years than Al. Al was potbellied with skinny legs, sparse body hair, and pasty-white skin. Joel was immensely overweight with a reddish complexion and abundant body hair. Al paid me to do both him and his brother that night (sequentially, of course). When I confided to them that Pam was actually considering an apprenticeship with me and wanted to get an idea of what might be expected of her, they happily agreed to let her watch. She even crossed her heart and swore to allow Al and Joel to be her first two clients should she decide to go into my line of work.

"It wasn't as gross as I thought it would be," she admitted afterward as we climbed the stairs to our room. "It seemed—oh, I don't know—friendly. At least a lot friendlier than I would have expected."

"I try to keep it friendly. To me friendliness and professionalism go hand in hand. Most hookers don't know the difference between familiarity and friendliness. And I wouldn't know how to explain it in terms they could understand."

"You don't have to explain it to me. I understand completely. But don't you find some guys so crude and obnoxious you can't endure to have them touch you?"

"Not really. I'm pretty tolerant. For a brief time I can put up with anything that doesn't constitute outright abuse. And anyway, most of my customers treat me really well."

Pam unlocked our door and let us in. I immediately started peeling my clothes off to shower and get ready for bed.

"I like Al better than Joel," Pam mused. "Don't you?"

"I don't make a habit of comparing people. I try

31

to find something to like in everybody."

"You're probably a nicer person than I am."

"I'm sure that's not true," I told her. "I'm me, and you're you. That's all."

On Monday, while Pam was picking up her contact lenses and learning how to insert them, I went to the bus station to buy tickets for us to leave town. Where to go next was the big question. I discussed the possibilities with the ticket agent and finally decided on Victoria, simply because I liked the name. However, a half hour into our trip we had a brief layover at a small-town bus station directly across the highway from a shabby little biker bar called *Hog Heaven*. It wasn't even dark yet, but to judge from the number of Harleys

parked outside, the place was enjoying a brisk business.

"Let's get down here," I whispered to Pam. "That looks like a gold mine yonder."

And a gold mine it proved to be. I made more money there on a Monday night than I had made at the Lone Star Saloon on a Friday night. Of course, I started at four in the afternoon and worked till long after the establishment had officially closed. Somehow I even felt secure from the cops while I was inside there. In future I would always be on the lookout for other similar bars. Bikers enjoy a mean reputation, but they always treat me right.

Another venue I found especially attractive was the Kappa Alpha house. In every college or university town we visited, I'd pay a call first on this my favorite fraternity to see whether a private party could be arranged on short notice. Those sweet boys only ever failed to come through for me if some other big event was already scheduled for my only available time slot.

For the next few months, Pam and I crisscrossed the state and doubled back and learned which towns to avoid and in which to maintain low profiles. Everywhere I went I was hailed as *Pocahontas* and greeted warmly. I could walk into a cowboy bar in some town I'd never been in before and be recognized immediately. I had become something of a demimonde celebrity. But I rarely allowed any of my clients to meet Pam. I was fiercely protective of her. I loved her as a little sister. Nor had there ever been the least hint of sexual or romantic tension between us. We were best friends; that was all. Or so I believed.

"Have you ever been in love?" she asked me the night we arrived in Beeville. It was almost bedtime. I was brushing my teeth. She was sitting on the toilet peeing.

33

I laughed at her question. "I'm not the kind of girl who falls in love."

"I am."

"I would have guessed as much. How many times have you been in love?"

"Just once." She wiped and flushed, then stood and pulled her panties up. "This is the first time."

I glanced at her in the mirror. She was gazing at me with cow eyes. Distinctly discomfited, I rinsed my toothbrush and put it away, then stepped aside to give her access to the lavatory. I said nothing; I had no idea what to say.

"Are you upset with me?" she asked as she washed her hands. "Should I not have told you?"

"No, it's okay."

The thing was, her declaration had taken me totally by surprise, and I simply couldn't decide how I felt about it. I cared for her too much to be angry at her. But was I even capable of returning the kind of adoration I could now read in her face? In my entire life I had never experienced infatuation, romantic longing, or even sexual arousal. I had believed that I was immune to all such foolishness. And yet the more I thought about it, the more I liked the idea of sharing that kind of intimacy with my first real friend. Slowly and deliberately Pam dried her hands, then carefully hung the towel on the hook beside the lavatory.

"I'm going to kiss you now," she warned me.

This was my chance to say, "Please don't." But I kept my silence. I wasn't at all certain I wanted her to kiss me, but neither was I sure I didn't want her to. My heart was pounding fiercely, so nervous was I.

Taking my face gently but firmly between her hands, Pam made good her promise.

Oh, but it was a sweet and tender kiss! I melted

inside. And in that moment my dormant libido awoke full-blown, and I learned for myself what raging desire felt like. My hands were all over Pam's body. I touched every part of her, and dear God, she felt good! Apparently Pam was possessed of the same need to touch all of me. We quickly stripped each other naked and raced to the bed, hers being the closer to the bathroom door. None of my past experience was the least bit helpful now. I felt myself to be as much a virgin as Pam. But we were fast learners. Such pleasure we gave each other that night! I reached orgasm first, and it was my first ever in eighteen years of living. Pam, seeing my face contort is exquisite agony, could no longer hold back her own climax. But that was not the end by any means. We scissored each other and tribbed. We did sixty-nine, we fingered each other's vagina, and we sucked each other's clitoris. We came over and over again that night until at last we were completely spent.

"If men get even half as much pleasure from fucking me as I get from making love to you," I whispered in her ear, "then I need to start charging more."

"You can't do that, darling. No one but a billionaire has enough money to pay you what you're worth. Think of all the poor bastards you'd be depriving."

We slept naked in each other's arms for perhaps two hours, then got up and showered together. Standing under the warm downpour, we slathered each other's body with scented suds and tenderly made love again. We were gloriously happy. How could I never before have suspected how wonderful it would be to be in love?

"Let's head back to Los Gatos, where we started," Pam suggested. "I want to go to work with you. I want us to do everything together from now on."

35

I wasn't sure that this was such a good idea. I tried to discourage her, but her resolve was firm. If the oldest profession was good enough for me, she insisted, then it was good enough for her. We were two of a kind. Henceforth, she meant to contribute to our partnership as much as I did. However, she had promised the Gibson brothers that they could be her first two clients, and she intended to fulfill that promise. I could only admire her integrity. There is a line in "The Cremation of Sam McGee" that perfectly expresses my attitude regarding the sacredness of one's given word: "A promise made is a debt unpaid." This is one of the mottoes by which I live, and I was extremely gratified to realize that Pam felt the same way.

CHAPTER V
In Which Pam Makes a Strange Confession

A medicine bag is a Native American talisman worn on rawhide thongs around the neck like a pendant necklace. While every Indian nation has its own traditions and its own language, medicine bags are common to all tribes. These little leather pouches typically contain a collection of small objects that hold some special meaning for the wearer. Cowrie shells, animal teeth or claws, arrowheads, smooth stones, and Indian-head coins are the items most commonly found in medicine bags. My own medicine bag, the one I had worn next to my heart since kindergarten, contained examples of all these items. The bag itself with only one object inside (an obsidian arrowhead) had been given me by my paternal grandmother on the occasion of my fifth birthday. Over the years I had added the other objects myself. This bag was, without doubt, my dearest possession. It meant more to me than all the wealth in the world.

Lying in bed naked with Pam, I was so filled with tender feelings for her that I removed the bag from my own neck and placed it around hers. Pam herself had never worn a medicine bag. Her mother, since taking the Jesus path, had deemed medicine bags to be symbolic of paganism and had forbidden Pam to wear one. My own mother had felt the same way, but her superstitious fear of the medicine bag's power had kept her from depriving me of its protection. Now I passed that protection on to Pam, who fully understood the significance of my gift. Tears of joy sprang to her eyes, and she covered my face with kisses.

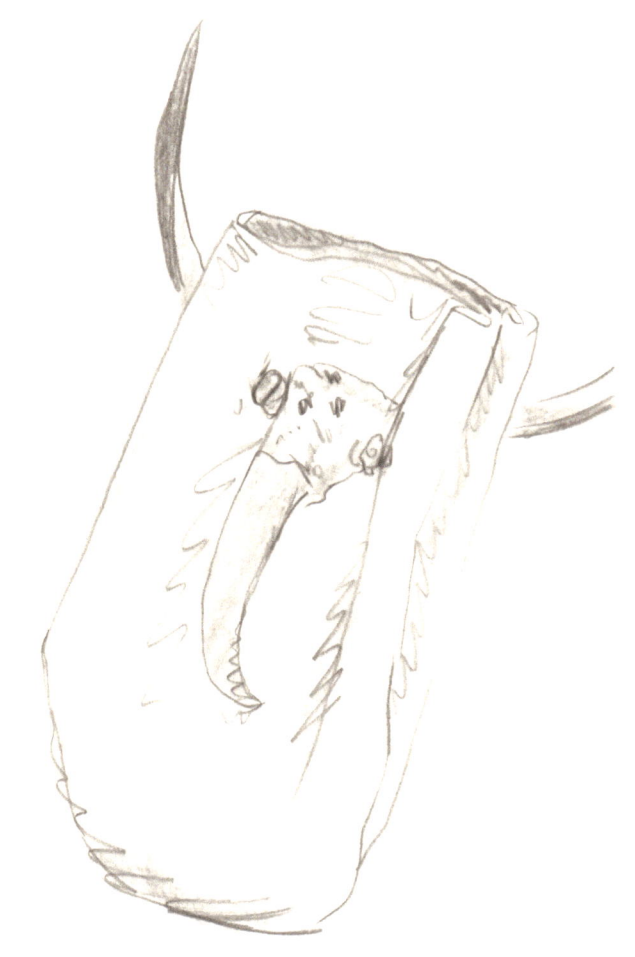

"We have to get you a new bag right away," she told me. "Without this, something really bad could happen to you."

"Or I could just stay close to you and enjoy the protection you get from this one."

"I like that idea. But I'm still going to buy you a new bag when I start earning my own money."

We had made plans to return to Los Gatos early the following week. But before that, I had a *pachanga* to attend at a big ranch near the town of Alice.

A *pachanga* is a *fiesta* of sorts. This particular *pachanga*, taking the form of a barbecue supper and beer bash, was to be a bachelor party for a young man soon to be wed. My rôle in the affair was to seduce the groom into having sex with me in front of all the other guests. When that was accomplished, I would be welcome to organize a gangbang. The best man would be bringing cases of condoms to pass out as party favors.

Pam was determined to accompany me, but only as a witness. She could make herself useful by collecting payment from those who lined up to fuck me. Pam had recently ordered a miniaturized credit-card scanner that attached to her smart phone. Tonight she would be using it for the first time. I had been paid in advance (and generously) for pleasuring the guest of honor, but the big money was what I might make afterward. Pam and I planned to arrive late, when the drinking had already been underway for an hour or more and when the food was just about ready to be served. We would then dine with the guests, who would be told only that we had brought the evening's entertainment. No one, save the best man, was to know until the time came exactly what that entertainment might entail.

"Everyone will assume you're a hootchy-kootchy dancer," predicted the gentleman who hired me, "or a stripper or something of that nature."

Darkness had fallen when at last we were handed paper plates heaped with *cabrito* (goat meat), refried beans, guacamole, pickled peppers, and flour tortillas. We were offered beer as well, but declined, even though there was nothing else to drink. We sat on the tailgate of someone's fancy King Ranch pickup to eat. I had imagined this party's taking place at a nice *hacienda* with outdoor tables and chairs and Chinese lanterns strung between the trees. The truth was nothing like that. We were miles out in the wilderness with only a bonfire and several dozen pickups circled around it. *Tejano* music blared from an old-fashioned ghetto-blaster. Pam and I were the only females present. Even the cooks were men. Pam and I were also the only non-Spanish-speakers, but we had no difficulty understanding what was being said to and about us. Whatever the language, men always say the same sort of things.

The soon-to-be groom was a handsome young man of perhaps thirty years. He appeared to be quite prosperous. He was well dressed and smelled heavenly. An ostentatious gold-and-ruby ring glittered on his right hand. His name, not that it really matters, was *Adán Ramos*. He was slightly inebriated and put up only token resistance when I came on to him. The crowd roared its approval as he achieved penetration, then cheered again when he climaxed less than two minutes later. But their enthusiasm was even greater when I offered them the opportunity to drink at the same well as had the young Mr Ramos.

Tonight I set no time limit. I had come to realize that such a restriction really wasn't necessary. A little squeeze, a little touch, and I can precipitate a quick orgasm in any man. I used to consider this a dirty trick, but for these gangbangs, with my rates so drastically reduced, it's pretty much a necessity. And no one seems to mind.

Pam found the events of the evening far from intimidating. Indeed, she was quite exhilarated. I believe she was actually eager now to become the object of worship, as I was tonight. "I used to think it must be awful for you to have to endure being mauled by so many men. But now I can see it's not an ordeal at all. It's like you're a goddess, and they are your devotees."

"I guess that's about right."

"I nearly came tonight just watching. Do you ever get so excited you have an orgasm while they're screwing you?"

"I don't get excited when I work, at least not in a sexual way. I've never once been turned on, even a little bit. You are the only person who's ever got me hot or given me a climax."

"I'm afraid I might come when I don't want to. Will you be cross with me if I do?"

I smiled tolerantly. "I'll never be cross with you. And anyway, why would you not want to come?"

"I want to be like you and only have orgasms with the one I love, but I'm not sure I can hold back."

"Then go for it. Enjoy it fully. You have my blessing."

"For real? Are you sure?"

"Listen, Pam, I don't choose not to get turned on by the men I service. They just don't do anything for me. That's all. If I could look forward to an occasional orgasm in the course of a night's work, I should consider that a huge bonus. But it wouldn't make me fall in love with the man who got me off. My heart belongs to you and only you."

"Forever and always?"

"Cross my heart and hope to die."

"But what if you found out I'd done something really, really terrible in my past?"

The thought of sweet, innocent little Pamela's ever having done anything bad enough to shock me was absolutely laughable, and I said as much to her.

"You don't know me half as well as you think you

do. The only reason I had to leave home was that I'd committed an act so unspeakable I could never be forgiven."

"I think you'd better tell me. Then I can say to you, 'It doesn't matter, Pam. I still love you.' And you can quit worrying that I'll find out by accident. That is what you're concerned about, isn't it?"

Tears formed in Pam's eyes. She nodded mutely, then covered her face with both hands and gave way to uncontrolled sobbing. I held her in my arms and let her cry herself out, which process took about five minutes. When at last her tears subsided, I again urged her to make a full confession.

"Do you know what an English mastiff is?" she asked me.

"Some kind of dog, right?"

"Yeah, a really big dog. As big as a calf, I mean. I used to have one. I got him when he was just a little puppy, and he was so cute you'd never have imagined how huge he was going to get someday. His name was *Poochie*, and I loved him with all my heart. He was my best friend in the whole world. He slept on the floor right beside my bed. And I was the only one who took care of him. I groomed him and fed him and kept his water bowl fresh, and every day I took him to the park to play." Pam took a deep breath. Clearly we were coming to the part she dreaded to tell. "Often in the park there were girl dogs that Poochie tried to have sex with, and even when they would stand still for him, he was too tall for them. He could never get his thingy inside them. I felt very sorry for him."

"So you had sex with him yourself," I giggled. "Is that it?"

Pam nodded shyly. "The first time he tried to mount me, it was almost bedtime and I had just come out of the shower. In fact, I was still naked when I got down on my knees to reach under the bed for my house shoes, where I had kicked them accidentally. And that's when he took me completely by surprise.   I whirled around and slapped the shit out of him, which was the only time I ever hit him, and afterward I felt really bad for having done so. He had no way to know that what he was doing was naughty."

"He was just being male," I agreed. "This is what Nature compels males to do, whether they happen to be dogs or men or dung beetles."

Pam smiled sheepishly, relieved that I was being so understanding. "I tried to make it up to him by being super nice and giving him extra hugs, patting and stroking him all the time. Also, I resolved that if it ever happened again, I wouldn't be so quick to react negatively. But it seemed like maybe he'd learned his lesson or else he had lost all interest in having sex with me."

"So were you relieved or disappointed?"

"I regretted having hit him and I wanted the chance to undo my injustice to him. So finally one night I got naked and bent over my bed and invited him to get on me. He was a bit reluctant, but I coaxed him, and eventually he did as I asked. I mean to say, he went all the way with me."

The mental image of Pam having sex with a dog was so ridiculous, I started laughing and couldn't stop. I literally rolled in the floor and held my belly. In my whole life I had never before laughed so hard. When at length I regained my composure, Pam resumed her narrative.

"After that I let him mount me whenever he felt like it, which to begin with wasn't very often. But on the third or fourth time, I had an orgasm with him inside me, and it felt so good that from then on I was hooked. I got him to do me two or three times a week. Till we got caught."

"How did that happen?"

"I suppose we were making too much noise and attracted my brothers' attention. I don't know how they managed to get the door open. I always locked it. But they walked in and saw everything. They were totally disgusted, and so was my mother. When Daddy got home from work, she told him what had happened, and he took Poochie outside and shot him dead. I tried to tell them it was my fault and they shouldn't blame Poochie, but they wouldn't listen. They said I would have to be locked up, put away. What I had done was not just a sin; it was a criminal offense. Of course, they couldn't report it because doing so would bring shame to the entire family. Instead, they'd just have to commit me to some kind of mental institution."

"I don't believe they could so easily do that."

"What difference does it make? Staying at home would have been worse. They'd never have let me live it down. They'd still be reminding me of it twenty years from now."

"So you ran away."

"What else could I do?"

"Sounds to me like they wanted you to run away, like maybe it was the only way they could avoid confronting an issue they were incapable of dealing with."

"Yeah, I think so too." Pam took a deep breath and let it out slowly. "And now you know. Do you still love me?"

"Of course. I don't even disapprove. To my thinking, what you did made perfect sense for you at that time."

"Thank you for being so understanding. I was terrified you'd be so appalled you wouldn't want anything more to do with me."

"It'll take a lot more than that to drive me away."

CHAPTER VI
In Which We Return to Los Gatos and Pam Fulfills her Promise to the Gibson Brothers

Alice, Texas, is far to the south of San Antonio. I don't even recall how we ended up so far from our usual "stomping ground," but now that the *pachanga* was behind us, we were heading back to East Texas, where we felt more in our own element. Our immediate destination was Los Gatos, where Pam and I had first met and where Pam now meant to launch her own career as a woman of pleasure. Was she nervous? If so, she didn't show it. She seemed quite eager.

We had been on the road together for four months, she and I. We had been lovers for only six days. Getting down from the bus in Los Gatos felt like coming home. In celebration we went directly to the bus-station diner, sat on the same stools we had occupied before, and ordered hamburgers, French fries, and coffee. The waitress remembered us and commented on the fact that we were still together and seemed to be in much higher spirits than we had been the last time she saw us.

I gave the woman a conspiratorial wink and confided, "We're going steady now."

"She begs me to marry her," Pam fibbed, "But I'm not ready to settle down quite yet."

The waitress, clearly amused at our playfulness, went away shaking her head. Later, as she cleared our empty plates, she offered us dessert, adding, "No charge. It's on me."

This friendly gesture pleased us immensely. We accepted with gratitude, and we both ordered coconut cream pie. Pam's preferences in food (as well as in music and movies and books) are almost always identical to mine. In any case, we lingered and drank more coffee with our dessert and chatted with our new-found friend.

Her name, we learned, was *Kendra Wynn*. She was a bit older than we were (age thirty perhaps), slightly overweight (ten or fifteen pounds), naturally red-haired, and given to wearing a bit too much make-up. Nevertheless, I think most men would rate her sex appeal well above average. She had recently married her third husband, she told us, but long ago (after her first divorce) she had reverted to using her maiden name, and this she intended to continue doing. She had one child, a little girl of eleven years, but the father, Kendra's first husband, had custody. She did not explain how that unlikely circumstance had come about, but she hastened to add that she retained and frequently exercised visitation rights.

"I suppose you two are both students," Kendra speculated. "Where do you go to school?"

"We just finished high school," I explained. "We're taking a break before enrolling in college."

"What are you interested in studying?"

"Psychology," I answered truthfully. I had it in mind that when I retired from what I was now doing, I would go back to school and eventually become a clinical psychologist. I liked the idea of helping people learn how to be happy.

"That's cool. You must be very smart."

"I don't know about that. Just because I'm interested in psychology doesn't mean I'd be good at it."

"Well, I'd bet on you." Kendra turned to Pam. "What about you?"

"Me? Oh, I don't know. The only thing that really fascinates is architecture."

"I'll bet you want to build skyscrapers?"

Pam shook her head in firm denial. "I'm more interested in preservation and restoration. I love old buildings and I hate to see them torn down."

"Los Gatos has plenty of old buildings that need to be saved. You could have a lifetime career right here."

"I know. When we were here before, I noticed dozens of examples of frontier architecture, most in terrible disrepair. That's what got me to thinking about this in the first place."

"Good luck. And there comes the bus from Houston. I'm fixing to get really busy."

So we said hasty goodbyes, and as Pam and I got up to leave, I slipped a couple of twenties under my empty cup. Los Gatos had only one cab in service that day, or so I was told when I called the taxi company, and it was already engaged. If we wanted to ride, we would have to wait at least thirty minutes. So suitcases in hand, we set out afoot in the direction we knew the Gibson Arms to be. We had walked only a short distance when my favorite cowboy Brent Driskoll in his Ford pickup stopped and offered us a ride, which we gratefully accepted. I introduced him to Pam, and they shook hands very formally.

"How long do you plan to be in town?" he asked.

"Don't know yet," I answered. "Probably just through next weekend."

"Will you be at the Lone Star this Friday night?"

"I hope to be, but I haven't spoken to Lou about it yet. We'll just have to see."

"I still have your phone number. Is it okay if I call you sometime?"

"You bet, but only if you're ready to part with some money. My usual fee is two fifty."

Brent parked on the street in front of the hotel and carried our bags in for us. We both thanked him and kissed his cheek. Al Gibson was at the reception desk and seemed quite sincere when he said he was glad to see us again.

"You're going to be even gladder when you hear why we've come back."

"Oh, yeah? Why's that?"

"Pam here has decided to go into business with me, and she means to let you be her first client. She made her mind up a week ago, but she hasn't started yet because she made you a promise."

Timidly Pam put her two cents' worth in. "I hope you're still interested, Mr Gibson, 'cause I wouldn't want anybody else to be first but you."

"Oh, I'm interested alright. This is the best news

I've heard in ages."

"Where's your brother? I'm going to let him be second after you."

"Joel's busy in the coffee shop right now. We lost a cook and a waitress both this week. So we're a little shorthanded."

I nudged Pam. "Let's go up and take a shower and change clothes. We can talk business later."

Al carried our bags up for us. He had offered us a larger room than before, one with two beds, but we had asked instead to be put back in our old room. "Stupid sentimentality" is how I had explained the odd request.

Setting our bags down inside the room, Al handed Pam the key. "I nearly forgot. I've been holding your mail. If you'll stop by the office later and I'll give it to you."

Pam seemed genuinely perplexed. "Who'd be writing me here?"

"The bank," Al reminded her.

"Oh, sure. I forgot about the bank. I'll pick the mail up later. Thanks."

Pam had been buying money orders and sending them to the bank every week. We had intended before now to open other accounts in other banks. But somehow we hadn't got around to it. We also needed to come up with a cover story to explain all that money. We were happy to pay taxes on it, but we could hardly afford for the government to know that it was earned illegally.

We had briefly considered claiming to be speculators in antiques, but then we had no shop and no inventory. So next we weighed the possibility of pretending to be traveling masseuses, belly dancers, or even fortune tellers. I could just imagine myself reading someone's palm: "I see in your very near future a most-satisfying sexual encounter with a beautiful Indian princess." But could I bring it off without laughing at the absurdity of it all? Probably not.

We should already have been filing quarterly returns, but of this we were both blissfully unaware. We assumed that we had till the end of the year to decide how to handle the question of taxes. Before getting Pam to open that bank account, I had been off the radar as far as IRS was concerned. But I had never been able to accumulate more than about sixty thousand dollars without having it taken from me. Now the money was safe, but my criminal activities were in the spotlight. Sometimes there isn't any way to win. You just have to decide what the least objectionable way to lose is. The bank was beginning to seem like a bad idea, but there was no changing course now. I'd bought into this game, and I simple had to play the hand I'd dealt myself.

When Pam went down to collect her mail, Al prevailed upon her to make good her promise right then and there. I was taking a nap and would hardly miss her if she did not return right away. So she agreed and allowed him to lead her to his bedroom.

"Would five hundred be enough? I know it's going to cost me extra to be first with you, but five is as much as I can put my hands on right now."

"Five hundred'll be fine, Mr Gibson."

In fact neither Pam nor I had thought to charge extra for her premier performance. But Pam is a quick learner, and she was not about to pass up a two hundred fifty dollar bonus.

"I think he was more nervous than I was," Pam told me afterward.

"Did he feel that he got his money's worth?"

"I'd say so. He seemed perfectly content when I left."

"And have you made a date to do Joel yet?"

"I haven't even seen Joel. Maybe we can have supper in the hotel coffee shop tonight, and if he's not too busy, I can discuss it with him then."

"Pamela, darling, I'm very proud of you."

"Why? I didn't do anything you don't do all the time."

"I figured I'd have to go with you and hold your hand the first time."

"Actually, I didn't quite know how to begin; so I just let Mr Gibson do whatever he wanted to do."

"But he used a condom?"

"Oh, yes, I wouldn't have let him near me without one. I know how important that is."

Later that afternoon we walked to the Lone Star Saloon, and I introduced Pam to Lou. He could barely take his eyes off her as we made plans for two double gangbangs over the coming weekend. Those who had me on Friday could come back and have Pam the next night and vice versa. When our deal was struck, Lou took Pam into the backroom while I tended bar for him. The only patrons in the establishment at that time were travelers: one party of three men and a woman. They were all drinking Pearls. When they ordered another round, I brought the four beers, but I didn't know how much to collect. So they told me the price, paid me, and gave me a one dollar tip, which gesture, incidentally, I appreciated more than you can probably imagine. Don't ask me to explain.

As Pam came out of the backroom, she gave me a little wink. Right behind her came Lou, tucking his shirttail into his pants. His face was quite flushed; his expression, smug.

Pam's first day on the job proved even more eventful than we could have predicted. Chief Taggart stopped by and demanded a *ménage à trois* with her and me. He had taken steps to address his impotence. He was now on a high daily dose of Cialis, which seemed to have worked miracles for him. His general health appeared to have improved as well, and gone was his halitosis. Thank goodness for that final blessing.

Then after supper that night, Pam managed to get together with Joel Gibson. He was her fourth sexual partner (if we don't count the English Mastiff), it's true, but he was only her second paying customer. She was able to say (with technical honestly) that she had kept her promise to him.

"How do you feel now?" I asked her. "Are you glad you started down this road or sorry?"

"Glad definitely. I really like doing this. But I know what you mean now. The thrill isn't sexual. It's something else entirely."

"You didn't get turned on like you thought you would?"

"Naw, not a bit. It is exhilarating, but not in an erotic way. Watching was erotic, but doing it's not."

On Friday night at Lou's Lone Star Saloon, I was welcomed back as *Pocahontas*. No one knew my real name. But they all remembered me fondly. I was everyone's favorite redskin until I introduced Pam as *Little Beaver*. The crowd roared their approval, and more men lined up at her table than at mine. Even Brent Driskoll chose her over me. My feelings weren't hurt, however. He'd already had me, and I know how men are. A new girl is always more desirable.

The evening passed quickly, and after closing, we invited Lou have his pick of us. He chose me. See what I mean? He'd had Pam more recently, and nothing is more exciting to men than variety.

Here's a little hint to wives and girlfriends. I

know you aren't going to want to believe this, but it's true. Your relationship with your man will be greatly improved if you encourage him to go out frequently and screw prostitutes. They aren't going to take him away from you; they don't want him. And when he comes back to you, you will be the new girl.

CHAPTER VII
In Which Pam and I Face Misadventure on the Road

My monthly periods have always been very regular. Pam says hers used to be totally unpredictable. But strangely, from the very first month we were together, her periods began conforming closer and closer to mine. Now we start on the same day and finish on the same day. I don't know why this should be. But for Pam it's been a huge blessing. Even before we became lovers, she was counting this new predictability of her cycle as a marvelous bonus to our association.

In any event, we were both expecting to be wearing tampons next weekend; so there seemed no point in being in too big a hurry to move on to the next town. We could easily afford to enjoy a leisurely vacation here in Los Gatos. And the more time we spent here, the better we liked the place. We had come to consider the Gibson brothers real friends. Likewise, Brent Driskoll, whom we seemed to run into almost daily. Chief Taggart was about the most-agreeable policeman a working girl could hope to encounter, and as long as we attracted no unwanted attention from the more prudish elements of his town, he was happy to have us remain here. Then of course, there was the waitress Kendra Wynn. We had avoided telling her what we did for a living, but I had the sneaking suspicion that even if she knew, she might not be in any position to look down on us overmuch.

Brent failed to call for a date with either Pam or me that week, but every time we saw him, he repeated his intention soon to do so. We simply assumed that he had difficulty scraping together the wherewithal. Someone who did call was Pam's optometrist. He had now enjoyed quickies with each of us at Lou's place. But he longed for an extended double header with both of us, and he wasn't the least bit reluctant to cough up five hundred dollars for the privilege.

While we were always extremely circumspect about whom we gave our phone numbers to, there were a few in Los Gatos who could and did call us for dates. We invited them up to our hotel room only when there seemed no other place to meet. I was very concerned lest steady traffic in and out of the Gibson Arms should lead to widespread gossip about the goings-on there.

Of course, we still enjoyed a lot of leisure time, and Pam wanted to take advantage of the situation to make photographs of some of the old buildings in town. For that purpose she bought herself a sixteen-megapixel Nikon camera. Then I followed her around as she snapped hundreds of images.

"Photography could be your cover profession," I suggested.

"You're right. I should have thought of that myself. And then when we retire, I'll already have a legitimate business to go into."

"Pamela Pinto, architectural photographer."

"I like the sound of that."

Pam took pictures of me too: nothing risqué, understand, just ordinary snapshots. When we're not working, we're as unremarkable as any two teenage girls you'd meet on any street in America. Just to look at us, you'd have no suspicion whatever that we were hookers. We don't dress the part. And even for work, we don't wear outfits any sexier or more revealing than those worn by other girls our age.

The balance in our checking account (Pam's checking account, I mean) was now over a hundred thousand dollars. And she had bought CDs totaling fifty thousand. But she had been telling me for some time that she wanted to start putting money into other assets. She had been doing extensive research online. This week she opened an account at Scottrade and began buying stocks. I think that's what she told me. I like having money, but financial instruments and calculating investment risks and returns bore me to tears. If Pam is willing to figure out what needs to be done, I'm more than glad to let her make all our financial decisions. Oh, yes, she also rented a safe-deposit box, because she meant to start filling it with items like rare coins and stamps, heirloom jewelry, and anything with value for collectors, even comic books and baseball cards, about which I might actually know a thing or two. She assured me she would never tie up more than a modest percentage of our accumulated wealth in any one type investment. Diversification, she informed me, was the key to secure prosperity. I suppose she knows what she's talking about. Who would have guessed that becoming a millionaire meant having to deal with such tedious details? What a terrible life Warren Buffett must lead!

I'm joking, of course. I know that not everyone is as financially illiterate as I am. And most people wouldn't find it all that onerous figuring out how to multiply their wealth. But that's just who I am. I have ambition enough to earn mega bucks and the self-discipline not to poop it off on cars and bling and ridiculously unnecessary luxuries. But someone else will always have to tell me how to choose investments. I simply do not wish to be burdened with that responsibility.

The thing is, if I am to be completely candid, I secretly harbor the attitude that willfully acquiring money through investment or indeed through any means other than by one's own labor is less than fully honorable. I wouldn't argue that collecting interest or receiving dividends is absolutely immoral. It just feels a bit shabby to me. Mind you, I adjust my values somewhat to the culture in which I find myself living and trying to survive. And I'm certainly not fanatical in my unconventional beliefs about money. So if Pam wants to invest it where it will draw the best return, I'm not about to object. Just don't expect me to take an active interest in the process.

We remained in Los Gatos for almost two weeks. From there we traveled north to Bryan and from Bryan to Corsicana, then on to Palestine, Nacogdoches, Kilgore, Longview, Sulphur Springs, Commerce, Greenville, Denton, and eventually Wichita Falls before starting back south again by way of Waxahachie, San Marcos, and then New Braunfels, our final stop before hitting Los Gatos again. When Greyhound didn't go where we wanted to go, we easily found alternative transportation. Usually there would be small stage lines operated by independent bus companies. On a few occasions we even hitched rides with truckers. Our fame (or should I say our notoriety) preceded us. As *Pocahontas* and *Little Beaver*, we totally redefined the term *friendly Indian*. We were legendary, and our services were much in demand and greatly appreciated.

"Do you realize that we are now almost halfway to our goal of becoming millionaires?" Pam asked me as we rolled into New Braunfels. "This time next year we could be retired."

58

"Are you looking forward to your retirement?" I asked.

"It's up to you. I'd be glad to go on like this for years. I'm happier than I've ever been, and I'm having fun."

After checking into the Faust Hotel, we set out afoot to visit a restaurant we remembered from our previous layover here. New Braunfels has more really nice eating establishments than any other small city in the world, but the Red Rooster is easily my favorite and Pam's. On our fifteen-block walk, we were whistled at by guys in pickups and in low-riders. We waved cheerily at them, but we were too hungry to stop and chat as they wanted us to.

After giving the waitress our order, we thought we'd take turns visiting the ladies' room. Pam went first, but while she was gone, our meal was served. That's how fast it was. Then when Pam returned, I decided that I could wait to pee until after we'd eaten. We took our time and enjoyed ourselves. The food at the Red Rooster is what is stylishly called *new American cuisine*. But what we liked most about the Red Rooster was the ambiance. In my experience, the food one gets in restaurants is almost always good. Nobody ever opens a restaurant to serve bad food. So the thing that distinguishes one restaurant above others is almost necessarily the mood created by the décor and the quality of service.

We ate slowly, relishing every bite, then lingered for dessert and coffee. As we got up to leave, I reminded Pam that I still needed to duck into the ladies' room. She walked outside to wait for me on the sidewalk. When I came out, I found her chatting with Brent Driskoll, who had, it seems, driven over from Los Gatos to attend a livestock auction. Bumping into Pam and me was an unexpected pleasure. He asked Pam for a date and expressed regret that he didn't have money enough to engage both of us. Having the two of us together in his bed, he confided, would be about as close to heaven as he ever hoped to get.

"How long you going to be in town?" I asked.

"Sale's this weekend. I'll probably drive back on Sunday. Why? You want a ride?"

"We'll make it worth your while."

"Two for the price of one?"

I stuck out my hand to shake. "You got a deal, cowboy."

Brent took us straightaway to the Super 8 Motel, where he was staying. For two hundred fifty dollars he got double his money's worth. Afterward, he drove us to our own hotel, where he promised to collect us early Sunday morning for the return trip to Los Gatos. Then I called Al Gibson to let him know to expect us back. I wanted to be sure we could sleep in our old room.

Our weekend was hugely profitable. We did a double gangbang on Friday night at a cowboy bar and another on Saturday night at a biker bar. We were rolling in money.

When Brent picked us up on Sunday morning he was towing a long stock trailer full of white-face heifers. As we passed through the little town of Mexia later that morning, a farm tractor backed out onto the highway in front of us. Brent swerved sharply to avoid a collision, but in the process, he tipped his trailer over, seriously injuring several of the animals he had just bought at auction. The police came, and an accident report was filled out. Pam and I, as witnesses, had to give our names and phone numbers. When we were finally free to leave, Brent still had injured stock to deal with. He estimated that he might be detained another couple of hours if not longer. So when two of the bikers from the night before stopped and offered Pam and me a lift, we said *adios* to Brent and climbed on the backs of the hogs. Brent promised to drop our luggage at the Gibson Arms when he finally made it back to Los Gatos himself.

The bike ride was exhilarating. Wind whipped our hair, and the countryside flew by. It was my first time on a motorcycle, and I loved it. We sped through one small burg after another. I had no idea where we were; nor did I really care. I was content to hang on tight and enjoy the ride.

Flashing red and blue lights brought our odyssey to an abrupt halt. We were pulled over for excessive speed in the little town of Broken Wheel, which amounts to nothing more than a few scattered buildings along a farm-to-market road. As citations were being issued, our two bikers became more and more truculent in their attitudes. Officer Dorner (I always read name tags) returned to his car to answer a radio call, and while he was gone, I urged the guys to be conciliatory and polite, lest they antagonize the cop into arresting us all. I was pretty sure he was right on the verge of doing so already. A second police car arrived as Dorner stepped out of his car and started back toward us.

No one could have seen what was coming next. It was perfectly choreographed to take us by surprise. I witnessed it with my own two eyes, and yet I'm at a loss to explain how both officers managed to get their batons in hand without our even noticing. Approaching from opposite directions and acting simultaneously, they suddenly cold-cocked the two bikers, knocked them unconscious. Pam and I were open-mouthed. Such brutal violence was absolutely uncalled-for. Hands cuffed behind their backs, the two bikers were loaded into the back of Dorner's patrol car as Pam and I, similarly hand-cuffed, were roughly shoved into the back of the other car. Before we drove away, however, the second officer, whose name, I noticed, was *Cooper*, kicked both bikes over into the drainage ditch beside the road. The keys were still in the ignition switches.

We were taken to what must be the world's smallest police station. It consisted of a single room that served as both office and detention center. The four of us were herded together into an iron cage in one corner of the room. There were no other prisoners. The uniformed dispatcher, whose name I was unable to read, was a young woman not much older than Pam and me. She was the only other person present, and she was about to go off duty. She could book us and fingerprint us before she left, she said, but Dorner declined her offer. He hadn't yet decided what was to be done with us. When she was safely gone, Pam and I were taken out of the cell for questioning. Remember, there was only this one room. The bikers were meant to witness whatever was to transpire and to overhear whatever was to be said. At this point the contents of our oversize purses were dumped out on the desk in the center of the room. The more-than-twenty thousand dollars Pam and I had between us looked mighty suspicious to the two officers.

"We're gonna have to confiscate this," Dorner informed us

Dozens of packs of Trojans scattered among the twenty-dollar bills didn't seem to merit his notice.

"That's our money," Pam objected. "We don't even know those guys. They just gave us a ride."

"The thing is, sweetie, it don't matter who it belongs to; if it's drug money, we gotta hold on to it."

"It's not drug money. We don't sell drugs."

"Then maybe you'd like to explain where all this

money came from."

I tried to signal Pam to cool it, but she was indignant and not in any mood to heed my warning. Still, she knew better than to admit to our having earned the money on our backs.

"That's none of your business."

"Bend over the desk."

"What?!!"

"You heard me. Bend over the desk. Put your hands right there and don't move 'em." He glanced at me. "You do the same over there."

They patted us down then, taking considerably more liberties than was really necessary. I have felt less violated being felt up by six or eight drunks at one time. Cooper relieved me of my Bowie knife, of course, but they found no other weapons on us and no drugs. Yet they required us to maintain our uncomfortable position.

"Maybe we ought to do a strip search," Cooper ventured.

"Oh, I believe a cavity search is what's called for," Dorner said.

"Like hell it is!" Pam whirled about only to be met with a vicious backhand blow that knocked her to the floor.

I bit my lip and resisted the urge to fly to her defense. Instead, I watched helplessly as she was rudely hauled to her feet again and forced to resume her previous pose. Her nose and her lip were bleeding. Even when Dorner lifted Pam's skirt and pulled down her panties, I said nothing. Moments later, I felt my own skirt come up and my panties come down.

"There are condoms on the desk," I reminded them. I wasn't sure whether they themselves had yet decided what they were going to do to us, but I had no doubt whatsoever that rape would be the eventual outcome. Might as well get it over with. "I'm sure you don't want to leave any DNA evidence."

"That's very obliging of you," Cooper said. He walked to the front door and threw the deadbolt. When he returned he picked up a condom pack and tore it open.

Dorner, standing directly behind Pam, already had his pants down and was unrolling a Trojan onto his erect penis.

They fucked us in the ass, and they fucked us hard. Damn, but it hurt! I thought I was used to anal sex. I had been done that way many a time before, but always more gently and with lots of K-Y jelly. Today, we had only the modest lubrication that came packaged with the condoms. Pam, who was still a virgin by the backdoor, found the experience unbearable. She passed out at the initial penetration and collapsed face down on the desk. Dorner kept right on humping till he came. I felt Cooper climax in my ass moments later. Afterward, I was allowed to attend to Pam. She revived pretty quickly.

"I think what we're gonna do," Dorner announced generously, "is let ya'll off with just a warning." He took a set of oversize brass keys from the desk drawer into which he swept all our money, and with those keys he opened the cell door to let our companions out. "Now, get your sorry asses outa Broken Wheel. And don't come back. Never."

In silent shame, the four of us hiked the mile and a half back to where we had left the motorcycles. Happily, there being no water in the drainage ditches, the bikes had incurred only cosmetic damage. We wasted no time putting distance between ourselves and this wretched place.

CHAPTER VIII
In Which Pam Acquires a Weapon and I
Make a Whirlwind Trip to Oklahoma

We rolled into Los Gatos a bit after six o'clock that evening. Our room at the Gibson Arms was waiting for us. Pam went straight to bed as soon as she had showered. She didn't even go down to supper with me. I figured that the unpleasant events of the afternoon had simply worn her out. I fully expected her to be back to her usual bubbly self by tomorrow. No such luck. She didn't go down to breakfast either, and she ate only a few nibbles from the chili dog I brought her at noon. She refused even to get dressed. It was as if all the life had been sucked out of her and she had become a mere zombie. Except to go to the bathroom, she stayed under the covers for the next three day. I brought her food at every mealtime, but she barely touched it.

Thursday morning, however, she seemed filled with purpose. She awoke early, got up, showered, and dressed before daylight. Together we walked to the bus station to have breakfast at the all-night diner there. Kendra waited on us. Only rarely had we not found Kendra behind the counter.

"Don't they ever let you go home to sleep?" I kidded her. "We've found you here at all hours of the night and day. Or is it that you just like this place so much?"

"When somebody doesn't show up for work, they call me first, 'cause I never say no to extra hours."

We ordered steak and eggs, hash browns, flour tortillas, and coffee. Not surprisingly, Pam was famished. I was glad that her appetite had returned.

"You got a new knife," Pam observed.

"That was my first order of business Monday morning. I feel naked without one."

"I want one too. Will you help me pick it out and teach me how to use it?"

"Sure, but only if you promise not to pull it on a cop. You have to let the police have their way. That's one of the rules of the game."

"Not this time, baby. I'm going to get that money back."

"Come on, Pam. Don't talk crazy. That money's long gone."

"I mean it, Jade. We earned it fair and square. I'm not letting those bastards keep it."

"Pam," I reasoned, "they've probably spent it already."

"Then I'll have their peckers to add to my medicine bag. They're not getting away with ripping us off that way."

I let the issue pass without further discussion. I certainly had no intention of allowing Pam to go off on such a foolhardy mission, but there seemed no point in continuing to argue at this time. For the moment, her mind was clearly made up. Nothing I could say would dissuade her. I could only hope that her righteous zeal would eventually give way to better judgment.

Neither my sheath knife nor the one we picked out that day for Pam could properly be called a *Bowie knife*, even though I sometimes refer to them that way. A real Bowie knife, a weapon fashioned after the one made famous by the frontiersman James Bowie, would be much too heavy for Pam or me to wield effectively. Indeed, to my eyes, a genuine Bowie knife appears only slightly smaller than a cutlass. Our knives are a fraction that size. After all, we have to be able to conceal them in our boot tops.

"Never threaten anybody with your knife," I warned Pam. "Pull it out only when absolutely necessary, and then draw blood as quickly as possible. The element of surprise is on your side. But surprise is an advantage you can lose mighty quickly if you're not prepared to be vicious enough. Attack, attack, attack."

"Vicious but not deadly, right? Just make him suffer."

"That's right. You're a fast learner."

High winds and a seemingly endless string of thunderstorms kept the crowd at Lou's place thin that weekend. Even so, we were able to bank a few thousand dollars on Monday morning. Still, it was much less than Dorner and Cooper had taken from us eight days earlier, which fact only served to renew Pam's determination not to write the loss off, but to either recover the loot in full or make the culprits pay with what they valued most. I could see no way such a quixotic adventure might end satisfactorily for us. To buy time in which I hoped Pam might lose her enthusiasm for righting wrongs, I agreed to devise a plan of action. In return, she promised to hold off doing anything on her own, "but only for a couple of weeks, Jade. I won't wait any longer than that."

Based on Channel 13's long-range prediction, we could expect bad weather to continue for at least another ten days. That meant business would be poor. Like it or not, this was the right time for me to return to Oklahoma to fetch my identity papers. I invited Pam to accompany me, but she declined. She would be waiting for me, she said, at the Gibson Arms when I got back.

Seeing my mother again was considerably less awful than I had expected it to be. I still didn't love her, but no longer was she able to make me feel guilty for not loving her. I could see her clearly for the self-righteous bitch she had always been. Her only need for other human beings is to help her feel superior in her piety. And she certainly has nothing to give in return. She did, however, produce my birth certificate when I asked for it and also my Social Security card. I thanked her politely, for I do believe that it is important always to exercise good manners. Then I said good bye. I was in her home for fewer than twenty minutes. I have no intention ever of returning.

I was back in Los Gatos late the following day. I had been gone only seventy-two hours, but I was already missing Pam terribly. So imagine my disappointment to find that she was not waiting for me as expected. A note left on my pillow indicated that she had gone to Austin for a date with one of her regulars. And while she was there, she meant also to explore a possible business opportunity she thought I would find very appealing. In the meantime, she had left me a thousand dollars in a sealed envelope in case I were running low on funds.

With Al Gibson I negotiated a new arrangement whereby this our favorite room was to become ours exclusively. Even if we were to be away for weeks or months at a time (as we often were), this room would never be rented out to others. We would be able to leave some of our possessions here, for we were now accumulating more odds and ends than we could easily carry with us when we traveled. And there might be other times in the future when Pam and I became separated. Henceforth, we would have a home to come back to, not just a rendezvous point. With Al's blessing, I repainted the walls of the room a dusty blue and the woodwork a rich cream color.

"This is beautiful," Al exclaimed when I showed him my handiwork. "I wish I could afford to repaint throughout. Now that I've seen your color scheme, that's how I'd like to do all the rooms and maybe something similar on the outside."

"Pam's the real genius behind this. She picked out these colors ages ago and then didn't have the nerve to ask your permission to repaint. I thought it would be nice to surprise her when she gets back."

"I like it."

"Pam says if the hotel isn't totally refurbished in the next few years, it'll be a write-off. Is that true?"

"Pretty close. When I retired from Halliburton ten years ago, I bought this old hotel at a bargain-basement price. I had big plans then to turn it into a stylish inn for vacationers. My savings were considerable and should have been more than enough to do all the work that needed to be done. Then I was diagnosed with cancer before we even got started. For the next three years I was fighting for my life. Joel gave up a good job with Amtrak to cover for me while I was in hospital. But medical bills ate up my savings. Still, the hotel was making a pretty fair return; so I had hopes that in a few years I could get enough ahead to re-paint and re-roof and so forth. Unfortunately, business has been in steady decline ever since, as has the condition of the hotel. Now I can barely keep up with the absolutely necessary repairs just to stay in business."

"How much would it take? Would you consider letting us invest in the hotel?"

Al smiled tolerantly. "More than you have, I imagine."

69

"Then maybe you don't have enough imagination." I always get a little testy when someone dismisses me so casually.

"I'm sorry, Jade. Please don't be offended. I didn't mean to insult you. I don't think you realize how much we might be talking about."

"How much? Millions?"

"No, not millions, but a lot: thousands just to repaint, then thousands more for a new roof. And that's before we even think about replacing the carpets and the draperies."

"Okay, then. Here's the thing. Pam makes all our financial decisions. So I can't say for sure we'd do this. But let me reassure you, Al, we can afford to."

Al's mouth fell open. The notion that a couple of teenage hookers might together be worth half a million dollars clearly had not entered his mind. "Are you serious?"

"I'm serious about being interested and serious about having the money. But you have to convince Pam that it would be a wise investment for us. Gather your facts and figures. Draw up a proposal or a prospectus or whatever you call it. Then be prepared to be grilled as thoroughly as if by Michael Bloomberg."

Later that day with Al's explicit permission, I ordered a local sign painter to create professional shingles for Pam and me to hang on the hotel veranda. Pam's would read *Pamela Pinto, Architectural Photographer*; mine, *Jade Stonecalf, Shamanic Counselor*. As long as you don't claim to be a psychiatrist or a psychologist, you don't need a license to charge people for advice. I might never get any legitimate business, but this was a good cover profession for me.

Then I went to the Texas Department of Public Safety and applied for a state-issued picture ID. With that I opened a bank account in my own name. I was feeling pretty high on my accomplishments for the week.

Two items on the television news that evening brought me abruptly back down to earth. In the first, Greyhound announced plans to convert its intricate bus network to a hub system with service to major cites, but not to the small town where Pam and I did most of our business. That was depressing enough, but the second item was even worse. It seems that Pam and I had inspired imitators. Two young women in Crockett had been arrested for prostitution. Other charges, including conspiracy, were being considered. A tavern owner was also under arrest, as were three city police officers, all charged with organized criminal activity. Names and mug shots were splashed across the screen. Happily, Pam was not one of those arrested. But I could forget about gangbangs. No bartender in the state would do business with me now. I'd probably have to go down to Houston and work a street corner. I was filled with dread at the prospect. There had to be a better way.

There was one other option. Now that I had proper identification, we could head up to Nevada and find work in a legal brothel. The idea was not terribly appealing, but better than working a street corner again. Storey and Lyon Counties in Nevada do allow eighteen-year-olds to work in brothels. All other Nevada counties that license and regulate brothels require the girls to be at least twenty-one. I didn't have to decide right away. But I was feeling the pressure. You can believe that.

Pam's optometrist called for a date that afternoon. Then a few other men called as well. I guess it took a couple of days for word of my being back in town to circulate.   Still, we didn't have enough regulars in this small community to support us for long.

When I ran into Brent Driskoll downtown, I asked him to give me lift back to the hotel. "There's something I want to talk to you about."

"What's on your mind, cutie?"

I told him about Broken Wheel and what had happened to the two bikers on the side of the road and what had then been done to Pam and me inside the police station. He was outraged, for which fact I was quite gratified.   And then I told him of Pam's unreasonable determination to get some kind of payback.

"She's right. You can't let those sons of bitches get away with that."

"If I can talk her out of it, that's what I'd prefer to do. But if not, then I need to make sure we have a plan that's not doomed from the start."

"And that's where I come in, right?"

"If you'll help me through this and do whatever's necessary, I'll give you a free lifetime pass. I should tell you, though, I don't think I'll be living here.   Still, wherever I am, you can come to me and I'll refuse you nothing."

"Forever?"

"Or for as long as you find me desirable. That probably wouldn't be more than twenty or twenty-five years."

"Somehow, I can't imagine my ever not finding you desirable."

"I want you to do a thorough recon for me. I need to know exactly where both those officers live and with whom. I need to know their schedules, what they drive off duty, who their neighbors are, who has dogs, and anything else you think I ought to know. Then help me plan an operation. And after that, you're off the hook. I'll do the dirty work myself. I'm not entirely without experience."

Brent smiled. "Yeah, you're tough. I can tell. I'm sure you don't need my help, but I believe I'll just back you up anyway. I'm not taking any chance of losing a lifetime of free pussy."

"Would you like a down payment?" I offered.

"Yes, ma'am, I believe I would."

CHAPTER IX
In Which Kendra Shows Herself to Be a Loyal Friend

I was beginning to be concerned about Pam's extended absence. What if she had got herself arrested? Way too many days had now passed without word from her. I tried repeatedly to phone her, but got no answer. I left voice mails. But she never called back. Finally, I decided to pay a call on Chief Taggart at his office and ask him to find out for me whether Pam were incarcerated someplace. I prefaced my request by letting him know that although I understood full well that the gangbangs at Lou's place were now a thing of the past, my door would always remain open to him. He made a quick computer search and assured me that no one by the name of *Pamela Pinto* was currently being held in any jail in Texas.

"Thanks, Chief. You're a real friend. Stop by soon so I can show you how much I appreciate this."

"Let's make it this afternoon, Jade. Around three if that's convenient."

Brent was now at Broken Wheel scoping out the situation there. He had not said exactly how many days he might be gone, but I rather expected him to be back soon. A former SEAL, he was well-trained for this type of operation, and I was actually starting to develop some zeal for the mission myself. The idea of taking revenge on Dorner and Cooper was, I have to admit, quite appealing. At the very least I meant to shove their night sticks up their asses. Let them find out what it feels like to be roughly penetrated that way. The only thing was, I didn't want Pam along. I was seriously afraid that she could not be controlled. With any luck maybe we could get this done before she got back.

So half my mind was hoping she'd remain in Austin or wherever she was till I could say "mission accomplished." The other half was worried sick for her. Every minute that passed without word was sheer torture.

At three o'clock precisely I let Taggart into our room. Promptness is a courtesy I really appreciate.

"Any special requests, Chief? Or shall I just be creative?"

Taggart scratched his head in that funny little way he has that always reminds me of Will Rogers. "Well, there's something I'm kinda interested to know. Maybe you could satisfy my curiosity, and then we could get down to business."

"Sure," I said. "Is this official police business?"

"Ah, hell, no! Just an observation of an oddity, you might say."

"Then come lie on the bed here, and let me

75

snuggle up beside you. I'll answer any question you have."

He complied without resistance. And as I nibbled his earlobe, he asked, "How come you and Pam don't ever do blow jobs? I mean, every other whore in the world would a million times rather suck than fuck. But not you two. Why is that?"

"Most girls in my line of work are lazy, uninformed, and unprofessional. They think they won't catch anything doing blow jobs; so they don't demand that their clients use protection. Fellatio is faster, cleaner, and easier to do than coitus, but it's not risk free. I'll do oral sex for you if you want me to, but you have to use protection, and that greatly diminishes the pleasure. Or so men tell me. They like to feel the last drops of semen being sucked out of them. With a condom, that sucking effect is pretty much lost."

"Nevertheless, I want to experience having my dick in your mouth."

"Your wish is my command." I rolled off the bed and reached for my purse to retrieve a flavored condom. I usually prefer banana. But I have other flavors too.

Taggart was very specific about how he wanted this done. He insisted on standing with me kneeling in front of him. I bet him seven dollars and fifteen cents (the exact amount he had in his pockets) that he couldn't make me gag. He did his best to win the bet, repeatedly driving in all the way to the back of my throat. Suppressing the gag response is not a piece of cake, but with practice and will power, it is possible. Taggart congratulated me on my victory, saying he had never before so cheerfully parted with seven dollars and fifteen cents.

"You've now had me every way but one," I told him as I tucked his penis back into his shorts and zipped up his trousers for him. That's called *service after the sale*, by the way.

"Something else to anticipate. You're one in a million, Jade. Before I met you, my life was almost unbearable. Now I actually look forward to every new day."

Taggart was back the following morning, and I assumed that he had returned in order to get intimate with my behind. Not so. He had news of Pam. "There's a Jane Doe unconscious but recovering from severe dehydration in Seton Southwest Hospital in Austin. The associated police report is one of the strangest I've ever read, but somehow I think this might just possibly be Pam."

I thanked him, and then as quickly as I could, I started throwing a few things into a suitcase. I wished now that I had bought a car and learned how to drive. I am never in a hurry, but today I was. I called a taxi to take me to the bus terminal, and for once it arrived promptly. Five minutes later I made the driver wait for me while I ran inside to see whether the Austin bus had left yet. It had. The next one would be hours from now. On the off chance that Brent had returned from Broken Wheel and not yet called me, I asked the cabbie to run me out to the ranch. As we pulled into the yard, I could vaguely see someone moving about behind the living-room curtains. I settled with the driver, grabbed my suitcase, and dashed up to the front door. But it wasn't Brent I had seen inside the house. It was Kendra Wynn. What the fuck was she doing here?

"Jade, what a surprise! Come in. How'd you find me?"

"Small town," I said evasively. "Everybody knows everything."

"So what's up? Why the suitcase?"

"I was on my way to Austin, but I missed the bus. Pam's in the hospital over there. At least I think she is. And I'm just so worried I can't think straight."

Kendra reached out her hand and wiped a tear from my cheek. "Well, you did the right thing to bring your problem to me. Give me two minutes to grab a jacket and lock the back door and we can be on our way."

In Kendra's car speeding toward Austin, my emotions got the better of me. I'm not a crier, but this time I simply couldn't hold back the tears. Worry, relief, and gratitude all vied for supremacy within me. "I can't believe you're doing this for me. You are such a good friend."

"If I ever needed anything, Jade, you'd be the first person I'd think to go to. You and Pam both."

"You don't have to work today?"

"I quit that job last night. With all the extra hours I put in for them, they wouldn't let me change my regular schedule with another girl in order to attend a program my daughter's going to be in next week. Ten days should be plenty of notice for a switch like that."

"So are you looking for another job?" I was scheming already to recommend her to Al and Joel for the hotel coffee shop.

"I'm taking it easy for a few days. After my daughter's program I can start putting in applications. The only vacations I've ever had in my whole life have been between jobs. Isn't that a hell of a way to live?"

I was still wondering about having found Kendra in Brent's house, but I couldn't think of the right questions to ask in order to clear up the mystery without giving away too much. Was Kendra now married to Brent? That seemed to be the case. But on the other hand, maybe they were cousins or pals or brother and sister. I do know that when I had last been in that house, there had been no evidence whatever of any female in residence.

We rode on in silence for another twenty minute or so, before Kendra asked, "Have you ever met my husband?"

"I don't know. Who is your husband?"

"Brent Driskoll."

"Oh, sure. He drives a Ford pickup, right?"

"Have you known him for long?"

"Longer than I've know you." Not entirely true, I admit, but longer than I had known Kendra by name.

"How well do you know him?"

"I'm not in love with him if that's what you're getting at. Pam is the only person in the world I've ever been in love with."

"But you came to the house today looking for him, not me. Right? I've been thinking how surprised you looked when I came to the door."

Time to own up, at least in part. "I was going to ask him to drive me to Austin. I would have offered to pay him. We're not close enough friends for me to ask such a thing without offering to pay."

A faint smile blessed her lips. She was satisfied. I had said exactly the right words. Nor had I lied to her. And yet I felt like shit. I wanted to tell her everything, but I thought it would be a mean thing to chance ruining her new marriage. If only I could count on her to be open-minded and forgiving (not so much toward me as toward her husband). Jesus! What a fucked-up situation! This was the first time I'd ever met a wife or girlfriend of one of my clients. And she's one of my dearest friends.

Silence prevailed for another fifteen or twenty minutes. Then as we entered the outskirts of Austin, Kendra resumed her cross examination. "There's still something you don't want me to know. Otherwise, when I came to the door, you would have said, 'What are you doing here? I thought this was Brent's house.'"

I took a deep breath and let it out slowly. "Look, I'll tell you the rest if that's what you really want, but I wish you'd believe me, it isn't something you need to know."

"Have you lied to me?"

"No, every word I've said has been the gospel truth. This I swear."

"Then I'll let you keep your secret for now. But if I ever ask you___"

"I'll tell you truthfully. I'll tell you right now if you insist on knowing. But I'd prefer not to."

She turned and stared into my eyes so long I worried that she wasn't paying close enough attention to the road. "I cannot for the life of me imagine what this could be about. I'll let it go for now, but only because you say so."

We found Pam conscious and drinking through a straw. She looked wretched. But she smiled at us as we entered the room.

"Look who brought me, Pammy. Here's Kendra Wynn. You'll never guess who she's married to: Brent Driskoll. Remember him? He's that cute cowboy with the Ford pickup."

Kendra leaned close and whispered in my ear. "She's in on it too? I think you really need to tell me everything."

I sighed. "Alright. Have a seat."

Kendra took the chair beside the bed. I sat on the edge of the mattress. For courage and support, I held onto Pam's hand.

Dreading Kendra's response, I plunged in. "The truth is, we're prostitutes, Pam and me. Brent's one of our clients. We didn't know he was married. The last time I was at the ranch, I'm sure he wasn't married then."

"But you knew him well enough to ask him to drive you to Austin."

"Like I told you before, I would have offered him payment."

Kendra's brow knitted as she chewed her lower lip. With the fingernails of her right hand she scratched furiously at the palm of her left hand. A nervous habit, I figured.

"Are you mad at us?" Pam asked.

"No, sweetheart, I'm not mad at you. And I'm not mad at Jade either. I'm just trying to decide whether to be mad at my husband."

"He seems really nice. I think, if I were married to him, I'd want to keep him, even if I had to overlook a few things."

"I'll bear that in mind." Kendra turned to me. "We aren't talking about past tense, are we? This is ongoing?"

I nodded. "He's very frugal. In ten months, he's only spent a few hundred dollars on us."

Kendra laughed. "You think that's the big issue here?"

"It would be for me. He's entitled to spend some money on his own interests and hobbies, isn't he? But if he were pooping off thousands every month, I'd consider that financially irresponsible."

"I get the feeling you count him a friend. Is that correct?"

"Not as close a friend as you, but yeah, we like him. I like him."

"Me too," Pam chimed in. "I like him."

"I'm glad for that. You respect him too, don't

you?"

"Oh, yes. I'd even go so far as to say I admire him."

"It's kinda funny. I feel like I should be furious, and maybe that will come later, but for the moment, I'm not bent out of shape at all. I'm just curious. Surely this isn't the typical response of an aggrieved wife."

"I don't think it's very helpful to think of yourself as aggrieved. Nothing we do is a threat to your marriage. And we always practice safer sex."

"That's good to know. I hadn't even got around to worrying about STDs. I'm still trying to work up a little jealous ire, and it isn't coming easily."

"We're not your enemies, Kendra. And if Brent's anything like most men, then probably he doesn't feel that he's cheating on you by coming to us."

"I should regard you as sex therapists or something like that?"

I shrugged my shoulders, embarrassed to admit aloud that that was exactly how I felt about it.

"When I was younger," Kendra admitted, "I used to do what you do. Never full-time, mind you. Just now and again when I needed extra cash. I mean, I didn't really consider myself a professional. It was just an easy thing to do. But I got busted when I was nineteen and did four months in jail. Then damned if I didn't make the same exact mistake again two years later. After that, I quit for good and took up waitressing. So you see, I do understand where you're coming from. I can even appreciate why Brent goes to you. You're gorgeous, both of you."

"Please, don't be too hard on him," I pled. "I'd hate for you two to end up separating over this."

"Oh, I'm going to let him make it. I just want him to start being more honest with me."

"Then it's up to you to let him know that he can trust you with the truth."

CHAPTER X
In Which Pam Presents Me with a New Business Plan

To tell Pam's story, I'm going to have to back up here. The morning after my departure for Oklahoma, Pam received a call from one of her regulars, a guy named *Napoleon Plum*. I've joined Pam and Napoleon in bed a couple of times myself; so I can tell you for sure, he's a thoroughly nice person and not the least bit scary. He's also very generous. Not infrequently has he slipped Pam an extra hundred dollars as a gratuity. By profession Napoleon is a videographer. He shoots TV commercials, music videos, instructional videos, documentaries, that sort of thing. He can call on plenty of professional models and actresses to appear in his usual productions. But when he decided to make a short *kinbaku* film, he needed someone far more adventurous and uninhibited than any of his usual performers would have been. In short, he needed a porn star, and he asked Pam whether she might be interested in filling that rôle. The compensation he offered was several times her usual fee.

Pam, totally enchanted with the idea and seeing all kinds of possibilities for a new career, readily agreed. She took the Greyhound to Austin that very day. Napoleon's girlfriend and business partner Dana Mars met her at the bus station and drove her directly to a studio that had been established in an old warehouse. There Napoleon was setting up the cameras and the lighting. The set, a traditional Japanese interior, appeared very realistic. Pam was introduced to her co-star, Daishi Nakamura, a very distinguished gray-haired gentleman of sixty or more years.

Now, Dana took her place behind one camera and Napoleon stood behind the other. This was just like a real Hollywood production.

"Lights. Cameras. Action!"

Daishi had the only spoken line. He requested Pam to undress in front of him. This she did slowly and deliberately, folding her clothes carefully and laying them in a neat little stack. Then she suffered Daishi to bind her with a brand-new cotton rope. He employed an intricate series of patterns and complex knots. Finally, he suspended her above the ground and commenced taking liberties with her person. Please understand, this was exactly as scripted. Pam had signed up for this.

The production was all but complete when Daishi's son Randy (a man of perhaps thirty-five years) burst into the studio out of breath to announce that Napoleon's teenage daughter had just been injured in a horrific car accident.

"Wrap this up," Napoleon shouted to Dana as he dashed toward the exit.

"The hell with it," Dana said. "I'm going with you." And she followed him out, leaving the two performers and Randy to shut down production on their own.

"What can I do?" Randy asked.

Daishi, now semi-nude, walked over to examine the two video cameras on their tripods. "The cameras are still running. Shall we finish this without the grown-ups?"

Pam, hanging uncomfortably upside down and not eager to even consider starting her ordeal over at a later date, said, "Go for it."

"Do you need me for anything?" Randy asked his father.

"You may remain silent and out of the way until we are finished, or you may leave now."

Randy chose to leave.

"How quickly can you come?" Pam asked Daishi.

"That is not the immediate question. To be answered first must be, 'How quickly can you achieve another erection?'"

Pam laughed appreciatively. "I'd give you a hand, but I'm sort of tied up at the moment."

Daishi stood there casually fondling Pam with one hand while playing with himself with the other hand, and they chatted amicably for perhaps another five minutes before he eventually made himself stiff enough to retain a condom. Then he penetrated her again. In and out he stroked, slowly at first, then more rapidly. Finally, approaching orgasm, he withdrew, peeled the condom off, and moved into position to ejaculate onto Pam's bosom. Her eyes closed, she felt the hot stream splash across her breasts. At that point, she involuntarily opened her eyes and was horrified to see her co-star clutching his chest, gasping for breath.

Daishi Nakamura died that day on the floor of the set, and Pam remained hanging above him for days. Inexplicably, no one came looking for either of them. Had not Fate intervened, Pam would surely have died as well.

When a drug task force comprised of local police and DEA agents entered the studio, they discovered none of the cocaine they had expected to find, but two naked and inert bodies, one already decomposing, the other barely clinging to life. Their search warrant named a completely different address, that of a warehouse directly across the street. Their mistake was Pam's salvation."

Initially Pam was admitted to hospital as a *Jane Doe*. However, a search of the studio shortly thereafter turned up her purse with her driver's license and Social Security card inside. Her chart and all records were then amended to reflect her true identity.

Naturally, all who shared responsibility for Pam's predicament were filled with remorse for having allowed her to endure such unnecessary suffering. Napoleon, who was still spending almost every waking minute by his daughter's bedside in the same hospital, made a point to call on Pam and to express his regrets for what she had been through.

"That's okay. I'm getting better by the day. How's your daughter doing?"

"She's conscious now and expected to recover. Thanks for asking."

When Napoleon left, Dana popped in with flowers, chocolates, and magazines.

Later that same day Randy Nakamura, grief-stricken at the loss of his father, also took the time to visit Pam in hospital and apologized abjectly for having left the studio that fateful day before she had been cut down.

"Don't worry about it," Pam said. "I don't want you to chop off a finger or anything for me."

"Oh, like Yakuza, you mean. No, I wouldn't do that. I'm more American than Japanese."

"I'm very sorry about your father. He was a nice man."

"I think he died happy."

"I believe I can promise you he did."

"Yes, that must be the best way to go."

When Randy finally said his goodbyes and left, Pam turned back to me. "We need to change professions. There are only two significant differences between prostitutes and porn stars. Porn stars make a lot more money than we do, and the police don't arrest them for the way they earn their living."

"Actually," I pointed out, "there's another difference, and to me at least, it's pretty important. Porn stars only do other porn stars. The guys we do, you and I, desperately need and genuinely appreciate what we do for them."

"True," Pam conceded. "I'd miss that. But porn's important too, Jade. Most guys we do have to depend on porn to help them get off when we're not around. And let's face it, we're not around for any one guy more than a few times a year."

"I'm not sure I'd like having to do what somebody else was telling me to do. I like believing that I'm in control of my life."

"How about if we had our own studio, and we didn't answer to anybody else? And all the guys we do on camera could just be regular guys. We could choose them from our fans, and I'll bet we'd have a million fans before we knew it."

"You're talking about doing this online?"

"That's the way to do it these days."

"And you think we can be successful?"

"I'd bet a million dollars on it."

"We don't have a million dollars to bet," I pointed out. "And that reminds me, I suggested to Al Gibson that we might want to make a sizable investment in the Gibson Arms. What would you think about that?"

"Is Al looking for investors?"

"He wants to refurbish, turn the old hotel into a fancy inn for tourists. But he doesn't have the money to do it. I told him he'd have to discuss it with you."

"What a neat idea! I'm really excited at the possibilities. Thanks, Jade."

"May I assume then that you're now prepared to forget about Broken Wheel? I mean, we have so many other things more important going on."

"No, I haven't forgotten, and I'm not going to forget. Have you come up with a plan yet?"

"I'm still working on it. This isn't going to be easy."

"You're not just stalling me, are you?"

"This is the riskiest thing I've ever done, Pam. I want to get it right."

"Okay then. While you work on that plan, how about if I work on a plan to get us out out of prostitution and into porn? Will you at least give it a try?"

"Yeah. I already figured out that we gotta make a change. If you come up with a good business plan, I'm in."

Leaving Pam well on her way to recovery, I headed back to Los Gatos on the bus. Brent had returned by now. And Kendra had already braced him about his relationship with Pam and me and possibly others. I can't quite imagine how that conversation must have gone. Somehow I can't see it as a fight. More like two people in love trying to come to an understanding they could both live with and live up to. I do know that at some point Kendra told her husband she could tolerate almost anything from him, except being left in the dark or lied to. So in the end Brent told his wife about the trip back from New Braunfels with Pam and me, the rape and robbery he was attempting to help us avenge, the nature of his recent out-of-town trip, and even my promise never to refuse him any sexual favor for as long we lived. In short, I found Kendra fully informed and up to date about absolutely everything. She even meant to participate in the Broken Wheel mission from here on out. Best of all, we seemed still to be fast friends. And the bond between her and Brent likewise appeared to be rock solid.

"So what's the situation in Broken Wheel?" I asked Brent as we three sat down together at their kitchen table.

"Good to go. I see no problem we can't deal with. Dorner has a dog that barks at his own shadow, but no neighbors closer than half a mile. The dog can be put down with a tranquilizer dart. Cooper's closest neighbor is about a quarter of a mile away. Both men live alone, never have visitors, rarely go out in the evening. They're both TV addicts. And they exist pretty modestly. If they've spent your money, I can't imagine on what. Neither one owns anything conspicuously new or expensive."

"How close together are the two men's houses?"

"Not close at all by the roads, but as the crow flies just a few hundred yards. I'll show you on the map. It's a fairly easy hike through woods and pastures. Have to cross a couple of barbed-wired fences though."

"Anything else?"

"Cooper keeps a strong box buried in a flowerbed by his kitchen door, digs it up every night, takes it inside the house to open it, then reburies it. His half of your money may be in that. Or it may be full of dirty pictures. I couldn't get a look inside without breaking the lock."

"I wish we could get the two of them together," I said. "Do you think that might be possible?"

"I think we'll have to deal with them one at a time."

"What worries me about that is that we don't know whether they split the money or whether Dorner still has it all."

"We'll hit Cooper first. That may be as easy as digging up the box. Otherwise, you can apply some pressure. I assume you'd enjoy doing that yourself. If we get satisfaction, we can leave him bound and gagged inside a closet with the door nailed shut. If it looks like we're going to have to go away empty-handed, we'll drag him with us to Dorner's house in case we have to have a second go at cracking him."

"What time does Cooper get in from work?"

"After six. He likes to have his supper in front of him on a TV table when his shows start at seven."

"How about if we're waiting for him when he gets home? We could already have opened the strong box."

"Sounds good to me."

"What else do we need to know?" Kendra asked. This was the first she had spoken.

"Let's all agree to a few basic rules by which we operate," Brent said. "First, no one carries a deadly weapon. The last thing we need is a fatality. I'll take a couple of dart guns and plenty of darts. And each of us will carry a pair of stun guns. Next to good planning, redundancy is the best insurance against a failed mission. And remember, even non-lethal weapons can kill if someone happens to have an allergy or a heart condition. So I'll carry a med pack equipped for every conceivable emergency from snake bite to cardiac arrest."

Kendra interrupted. "What could you possibly have for cardiac arrest?"

"An adrenaline syringe. But let's try not to create a situation in which we need it. Let's nobody use a stun gun or a dart gun unless the situation absolutely demands it."

Kendra and I nodded our agreement.

"Also, no one speaks in front of Cooper or Dorner, except Jade. And even Jade will not uncover her face.

No sense refreshing their memory of what she looks like. I want us to be as untraceable as a wisp of smoke."

Brent demonstrated a number of distinct hand signals by which we might communicate silently, and he made us practice them over and over. We memorized the map and discussed every possible contingency. We even practiced unarmed hand-to-hand combat. Kendra and I also learned how to use those dart guns we were not even expecting to handle. We had our escape carefully planned.

Acquiring boots and appropriate attire for Kendra and me was the next step in our preparation. I handed Brent a fat wad of cash to spend. Then we two girls gave him our sizes, and he drove to Houston to buy us everything he thought we would need. He assured us he would park blocks away from the sporting-goods store and walk there to avoid there being any possible record or his license plate at that location. I felt that such a precaution was a bit much, but I said nothing. The sloppy clothes and slouch hat he wore gave him an entirely different appearance than was usual for him. He did not want to be remembered, and if remembered, he especially did not want to be identified. I suppose, if you're going to engage in any kind of felonious activity, you really can't be too cautious.

On Tuesday the thirteenth of November, we were expecting a new moon. It was, therefore, on that day that Brent preferred to launch our operation. Nor would we even consider the weather. Wet or dry, warm or cold, we were going. Pam would be arriving from Austin around midday on the fourteenth. The timing could not have been better.

"I surely do admire how you've dealt with this," I told Kendra when Brent was on his way to Houston. I had made my mind up to remain at the ranch till the job was done.

"What else could I do? I didn't much want to lose my husband. And I sure as hell didn't want to lose my two best girlfriends. People make way too much of sexual fidelity anyway. What I would hate is to feel excluded from any part of his life."

"Do you experience jealousy when the three of us are together?"

"No, not at all. But the next time the two of you are together and I'm alone, my imagination will be working overtime to try to drive me crazy. But don't worry. I'll get over it."

"I wish I could tell you I'd never let him near me again, but I made him a promise before I knew you were his wife."

"That's okay, Jade. I actually feel really flattered that he still wants to be with me when I know he could have you every single night."

"That's the way to look at it. I'm just there to add a little spice to the mix. In any event, I'm really glad that we can all be friends."

CHAPTER XI
In Which I Learn that Revenge Is Sweet

About halfway between the towns of Broken Wheel and Dime Box, Brent had a pasture lease. At least that's what he called it. Actually, it was only a hay meadow. Depending on rainfall, he might be able to cut hay there as often as three times a year. There was no structure on the property, not even a barn or a shed, but this was where Brent meant to leave our getaway vehicle. There was one spot in particular, he told us, near the back of the pasture where a hillock would totally conceal a pickup truck from the view of anyone passing by on the road. This pasture was about three miles across country from Dorner's house.

At mid-afternoon Brent dropped Kendra and me on a deserted stretch of road in eastern Lee County. Then following Brent's careful instructions, we made our way through dense brush and a wood of scrubby little trees to a point directly behind Cooper's house. There we waited for Brent to drop the pickup off and hike back to us.

We were wearing jungle boots, and dark (but not black) clothes (each of us dressed differently). Brent had made sure that we didn't look anything like commandos. Gloves and balaclavas would remain inside our backpacks until we were ready to confront Cooper. After that they would not come off till the show was over.

The weather could not have been better. It was chilly and dry, but not too cold. For security reasons Brent would have preferred a steady downpour, but Kendra and I were grateful not to have to endure that discomfort.

At last Brent arrived, coming up behind us sopping wet from having waded East Yegua Creek. Not long after that, the sun went down, but dusk seemed reluctant to fall. Finally Brent, motioning us to remain where we were in the shelter of the trees, strolled casually across the yard to Cooper's back door and kicked it open. Now the house would be easy to enter. Brent knelt beside the concrete stoop and dug with his gloved hands in the loose soil. Momentarily he extracted what looked to me like an old army ammo box with a hasp welded to it. With bolt cutters from his backpack, Brent made quick work of the padlock that secured the hasp. For what seemed an eternity, I couldn't tell what he was doing. Eventually he laid the ammo box back in the hole and covered it again with earth. When he stood and came walking back toward us, he gave me a little thumbs-up signal.

"It's all there," he told me as he handed me a plastic bag of large-denomination banknotes. "Stuff it in the bottom of your backpack, and let's get out of here before he gets home."

"No," I said firmly. "I mean to put the fear of God in both these sons of bitches before I leave."

He didn't even try to argue with me. He just watched grimly as I stuffed the money into my backpack and zipped it back up.

"How much?" I asked.

"Twenty-two thousand."

Then they've ripped others off the same way, 'cause Dorner would never have allowed Cooper to keep more than half. He's the dominant personality of that pair."

"That means Dorner probably has at least another twenty-two thousand. Shall we try for that too?"

"Yeah. I think it's about time they found out what it feels like to be ripped off."

Rising road dust beyond the top of the hill told us a car was coming from the direction of Broken Wheel. Brent hurried back across the yard and entered the house by the back door just as that car pulled into the driveway in front. Five minutes later Brent appeared at the backdoor and signaled me to come inside. Kendra waited where she was. I found Cooper, in uniform, lying on the kitchen floor, his hands secured behind his back with a plastic zip tie. His equipment belt had been removed. It was nowhere in sight. I wondered where Brent had put it, but I didn't ask. I dropped my backpack just inside the door, then did a quick walk through to get a feel for the house. When I returned to the kitchen, I nodded to Brent by way of saying that I could take it from here. I very much wanted him on the outside watching for unexpected company. As soon as I was alone with Cooper, I delivered a vicious kick to his genitals. He fucking deserved it. While he groaned and whined, I knelt beside him and unfastened his trousers and tried to pull them down, but they wouldn't budge.

"Lift the weight off your hips," I told him.

"Why?"

"You want a blow job, don't you?"

The stupid bastard immediately complied, and I pulled his trousers and underwear down to his knees. Then I carefully tied a shoestring firmly around his penis as close to his body as I could manage.

"What are you doing?"

"I don't want you bleeding to death."

For a moment I thought he was going to faint; then he seemed to recover a bit. His belligerence even returned. "Who the fuck are you people?"

"I'm just a messenger," I told him, standing to survey my handiwork. "The message I bring is this: *Never steal from the Mafia*. It has to be written in blood, I'm afraid. That's one of the rules. By the way, your dick seemed a lot bigger when you had it up my ass."

"Jesus! You're that biker chick. Listen, I can get your money back. I still got my share, and I know where the rest is. But you gotta let me go."

I bent at the waist to withdraw my knife from my boot top. Then I squatted beside him and grasped his penis with my left hand. "Kiss it good bye, Cooper. I know you're going to miss it."

This time he did faint. Dorner probably wouldn't be this easy. He was just as corrupt, just as mean, just as stupid, but he had more grit. At least, I estimated that he did. At the sink I filled a glass with water to dash in Cooper's face. Within a moment he was sputtering and gasping. I knelt again, and in my softest voice, I asked sweetly whether he would do something for me.

"Anything. Just let me go."

"When I start cutting, I want you to let your feelings out. Don't hold anything back. You see, I really get off on the screaming. Would you do that for me?"

"Please." Tears were streaming down his cheeks.

"Christ, Cooper! You're fucking pitiful!"

"I can give you an extra thousand your bosses don't even need to know about."

"Oh, yeah? Tell me more."

"First you gotta promise to let me go."

"I could promise you anything. What makes you think I'd keep my word?"

"Look, I trust you. Why wouldn't you keep your word? A thousand dollars is a lot of money. We had no way to know who you were. Just let me go."

"Alright, if you do right by me now, I'll let you keep your little thingy." And just to show him I was no longer intent on emasculating him, I untied the shoestring tourniquet and put it back into my pocket.

Tears of relief flooded down his cheeks. "Shoe box, top shelf, bathroom closet. Thank you. Thank you. Thank you."

"Don't go away," I said and walked to the bathroom. There was indeed a shoe box, and inside was money, all twenties. It only took a minute to count it. With the box tucked under my arm I returned to the kitchen.

"Now let me go. I did my part. You got what you came for."

"There's only six thousand dollars here."

"Yeah, my share of what we took from you and an extra thousand."

"How come your share was only five thousand?"

"Half." He said it with such sincerity that I believed him.

"Dorner lied to you. He took more than twenty thousand from me."

"No, he wouldn't cheat me. We're partners."

"Where's Dorner's part of the money?"

"At his house. He keeps it at home. I can tell you where he lives."

"What makes you think he didn't deposit it in the bank?"

"He told me not to do that. He said if we put it in the bank, it might look like we were corrupt."

I laughed. "We wouldn't want anybody to think that, would we?"

Most American men are circumcised. Believe me. I know. That's why I found it particularly odd to note both Dorner and Cooper were still possessed of their foreskins. Well, I could fix that. I knelt and with my left hand I grasped Cooper's penis, which seemed to shrink up, as if attempting to retreat inside his body.

"Wait. Please. You promised. Damn it, you

99

bitch!"

Holding his foreskin between my thumb and forefinger, I pulled his penis taut. Then with a single slice, I circumcised him. Not surprisingly, he fainted again. There was a lot less blood than I had expected. I summoned Brent to nail Cooper into the hall closet.

Then we were on our way to Dorner's house to do the same thing all over again, but not before I put to use a can of red spray paint I had brought for the purpose of interior redecoration. On every wall throughout Cooper's house I repeated a scribbled message I had already delivered verbally:

Never steal from the Mafia.

Now, in case my reason for this vandalism is not entirely obvious, let me explain. Suggesting to Cooper that what was being done was being done in the name of the mob was a deliberate attempt to discourage his reporting the crime. Covering his walls with this kind of graffiti was meant to give him one more reason not to want investigators inside his home. I had a second can of paint reserved for Dorner's house.

I won't bore you by repeating all the same details as regards my interaction with Dorner. It went pretty much the same way. True, he was tougher, but not much. The worst part of the entire adventure was making our way through the darkness from Cooper's house to Dorner's. Wading the stream, we got wet up to our arm pits. Well, on Kendra and me the icy water was that deep; on Brent it was only a little over waist deep. Then it was alternately uphill and downhill with occasional brambles tearing at our clothes and scratching our faces and barbed-wire fences to cross. Once, I very nearly stepped on a snake. Fucking snakes give me the creeps. Spiders are the only thing I hate more.

As we approached Dorner's house, a dog could be heard barking within. When the back-porch light came on, we dove to the ground and lay motionless. The door opened and Dorner, gun in hand, stood silhouetted in the doorway. The dog continued to bark.

"What's out there, Rex?" we heard Dorner say.

Brent whispered to us, "No matter what happens, don't move a muscle. I won't let the dog hurt you."

Dorner was speaking to the animal again, but so low I couldn't understand. Then he loosed the collar, and the dog ran straight toward us, pulling up short about ten feet from where we lay in tall grass. It knew we were there, I think, but it was too cautious to come any closer. Dorner walked out into the back yard, but refused to go into the field beyond. The dog held its ground and barked. Dorner lost patience and went back inside. The moment the door shut behind him, Brent shot the dog with a dart. The dog yelped and ran away, eventually to collapse unconscious somewhere in the night.

"Stay here," Brent told us.

Then he moved around to the side of the house. The back yard was still flooded with light. I was really afraid. Dorner was alerted, and he was armed. For the longest time I heard nothing and saw nothing. Then the porch light went out, and Brent appeared in the doorway where Dorner had stood a few minutes earlier. He motioned me to come, and I did a repeat performance with pretty much the same results. I left with the other fifteen thousand, plus several thousand extra, but not before cutting Dorner as I had cut Cooper. Neither man was wounded seriously enough to absolutely require medical attention, unless infection should set in, and against that possibility I applied a liberal amount of hydrogen peroxide to my handiwork.

We did not nail Dorner up in a closet as we had Cooper. Instead, we tied him with ropes, but not so well that he could not in an hour or so work himself free. Before we left the house, I told Dorner where to find Cooper and how to free him from the closet.

The hike to the pasture where the pickup was parked proved much longer than the hike through the woods, but far less arduous. As exhilarated as I was, I believe I could have walked all the way back to Los Gatos.

When I managed to get Kendra alone for a moment later that night, I gave her the money from Cooper's buried ammo box, and I urged her to think of it not as community property, but as her own little private stash to be held for future emergencies or perhaps to start her own business someday.

CHAPTER XII
In Which Pam and I Become
Almost-Respectable Businesswomen

The caper to recover our stolen money was six weeks ago. Today, the hotel face-lift is well underway. A crew of painters is setting up scaffolding this morning, and a new standing-seam roof has been ordered. Likewise, carpet and drapery. A grand reopening is scheduled for March the twentieth, the first day of spring.

Kendra has taken over the hotel coffee shop and now runs it as an independent operation. Thanks to her friendly smile and adept management, the coffee shop is already vying with City Café for the title *most-popular eatery in Los Gatos*.

Pam and I have all but given up prostitution. We still service our trusted regulars when they call, but we no longer travel and we no longer do gangbangs in bars. Lou came by today and paid me two fifty to fuck him. Poor fellow! He used to get it for free. Chief Taggart still does, of course, and always will. I promised him as much, and I'm as good as my word. I do Brent for free as often as he asks. But Pam made him no such promise, and she does him almost as often as I do (charging full price).

To learn the porn business, I signed up for a photo shoot and a porn video with a classy outfit called *X Art*. They flew me to Florida and paid me ten thousand dollars for a few days' work. I was paired with their Mister X. I didn't like having to pretend that I was getting off; I had never faked an orgasm or even arousal, and I felt that doing so was tacky. I think part of my appeal has always been my honesty, my genuineness. But the director patiently pointed out that I was now an actress. Acting and pretending are one and the same, and the script called for me to climax before my partner. So I did (or seemed to). But I wasn't very happy about it, and I shan't do it again.

After I got back to Texas, Pam and I did a series of three fine-art nude videos for Napoleon Plum (non-porn, that is). We offered to do them for free if he would but teach us everything we needed to know about the technical aspects of videography. He said he'd rather pay cash, his time being so precious, but we held out, and eventually he loaned us Dana to be our instructor.

She is a sweet, nice girl, and she even helped us pick out the right equipment for what we wanted to do, which was to start a membership site online. That site should be fully operational by summer. I hope you'll check us out. We intend to be quite candid about who we are, namely two prostitutes doing what prostitutes do. We'll service individuals as well as groups of all sizes. We'll do hand jobs, coitus, anal, and oral, anything you can think of, but always safely. And there won't be any pretense that this is about our own sexual pleasure. We have no intention of faking arousal. We won't groan or gasp when we're fondled or penetrated.

By the way, we intend to do all our shoots at Brent's ranch. In consideration of that fact, he and Kendra have been given a small but not insignificant interest in our production company. If we prosper, they will too.

Let's see. What else can I tell you? We're not taking on any new paying clients. But if you want a date with either of us, that's still possible. The first step is to subscribe to our site. Then simply let us know that you want to appear in one of our videos with us, and be sure to tell us exactly how you'd like to be pleasured. Or you can leave that part up to us. We've never disappointed anyone before, and we won't disappoint you. I promise.

A Sequel of Sorts

If you liked this book, you might also enjoy an eShort titled *Paxton Cole, Private Investigator*, in which Jade and Pam find themselves being stalked by old enemies.

An eShort, by the way, is a short story in digital format (in this case, Kindle). Quite inexpensive, it can be finished in one sitting, perfect for bedtime reading.

Audio-book versions of both *The Chosen Profession of Jade Stonecalf* and *Paxton Cole, Private Investigator* are also available.

About the Author

Trudy Lynn (Bootsy) Silverheels was born in rural Yavapai County, Arizona, in 1986. She spent most of her childhood in Arizona and New Mexico and her teens in Mexico City. She graduated from high school and university in Mexico before returning to the United States for graduate studies. She died in 2014. In her short career, she published but three works of fiction— this novella and two full-length novels, *Dusky Nightshade and the Little Heathens* and *Nuevo Biloxi* (co-authored by Damien Wynter)—and an erotic memoir, *Baring All*. But she left dozens of book and short story manuscripts in various stages of completion. One of these, *Coming Clean*, was published posthumously in 2015. Others can be expected to follow.

www.ingramcontent.com/pod-product-compliance
Lightning Source LLC
Chambersburg PA
CBHW050904180626
46814CB00007B/2883